JESSIE'S SECRET

DORENE MEYER

Norwa ....da

This is a work of fiction. Names, characters, places and incidents
are either the product of the author's imagination or are used fictitiously,
and any resemblance to actual persons, living or dead, businesses,
companies, events, or locales is entirely coincidental.

All Scripture is taken from the Holy Bible – New Life Version
© Christian Literature International.
http://www.christianliteratureinternational.org/
"Christian Literature International (CLI) is a non-profit ministry
dedicated to publishing and providing the Word of God in a form
that can be read and understood by new readers and the well-educated
alike... and at an affordable price. We invite you to learn how the NEW
LIFE Version unlocks the treasures of God's Word!"

Library and Archives Canada Cataloguing in Publication

Meyer, M. D. (Mary Dorene), 1957-
    Jessie's secret / Dorene Meyer.

ISBN 978-1-927410-07-3

    I. Title.

PS8626.E933J48 2013   jC813'.6   C2013-900698-2

Cover Design by Yvonne Parks

Printed and bound in Canada by Art Bookbindery
www.artbookbindery.com

Published by Goldrock Press
www.goldrockpress.com

Acknowledgments

Thanks to John Carlin for his true stories about the baby ravens and the information about "candle ice."

Thanks also goes out to the three editors who have assisted with this book at its various stages. Melva Zook read and commented on the original manuscript, Lisa Holliday did a substantive edit, and Audrey Dorsch copyedited the final version. Thank you so very much, Melva, Lisa and Audrey!

I will give you riches hidden in the darkness and things of great worth that are hidden in secret places.

Isaiah 45:3a

Chapter One

"Let her go."

The words were spoken quietly but with a confidence and authority that left no room for argument. Jessie's tormentors released her and turned sullen eyes toward the young man approaching them.

He wasn't any older or even any bigger than most of the group of teens surrounding her, but no one protested when he pulled Jessie's earphones off the ringleader and reached out his hand for her iPod.

Jessie bent to pick up her hat and tried to smooth her hair down a little before putting it on. The stranger handed Jessie her iPod and silently motioned for her to start walking.

As she hurried down the path, a flurry of speech rose behind her. Though she couldn't understand their language, Jessie could hear the disapproval in the young man's voice and the defensive tone of the group.

She had already covered some distance when he caught up to her. Jessie turned to thank him but fell silent as she saw the scowl on his face.

"You shouldn't be out alone so late at night!"

Gratitude forgotten, Jessie glared up at him. Though taller than she was, he looked to be about her age, maybe even younger. What right did he have to tell her what to do and how late she could be up?

"It ain't none of your business what time of day I go walkin," she declared.

The young man eyed her silently for a moment before asking, "You're a guest at the lodge?"

"Maybe."

He shook his head and began to walk away. "I should have just left you there," he muttered.

"No!" Jessie hurried after him. The words tumbled out of her. "Yes, I'm staying at the lodge. My brother David is getting married."

He stopped and turned around slowly. "You're Doctor Rodriguez' sister?"

Jessie nodded and attempted a smile. "I just got in from New York this afternoon."

He was looking carefully at her now. The light from the moon reflected off the snow, making the night seem almost like day. Jessie could see the young man's finely sculpted features, broad shoulders, and athletic build.

She turned a little, and the full light of the moon cast soft shadows across her face. Jessie knew the ivory cardigan she wore brought out the rich dark tones in her face and hair. The V-neck top and tweed pants were a perfect fit. Jessie smiled at the handsome young man, sure that his evaluation would lead to a compliment.

"Maybe my sister could lend you some clothes."

Jessie stood for an instant in shocked silence before spinning away from him, her long strides marking the distance between them.

He was just like that bunch that had been bullying her. What did he know? What did any of them know about designer clothes, living up here in the wilds of Northern Canada? She'd saved up three paychecks just for the tweed pants and had convinced herself and her mother that the "warm sweater" she needed for the trip had to be this Ralph Lauren original.

"You can't blame them for teasing you."

Jessie tried to walk faster, but her chunky-heeled shoes were more suited for sidewalks than for bush trails, and she almost fell twice.

"And you look kind of cold."

Jessie slowed down a little. It was true; she was cold. It was the end of April and although she knew she'd be quite far up north, she hadn't anticipated that it would still be below freezing at this time of the year,

The young man was beside her now. "You could borrow my jacket."

He was actually kind of cute when he lifted one eyebrow and gave her that lopsided grin. Jessie couldn't help but smile back.

He took off his jacket and handed it to her.

"Won't you be cold now?" Jessie asked, feeling warmer already as she slipped her arms through the thickly padded sleeves of the wool and leather jacket.

He shook his head and showed her the collar of another shirt beneath the hooded sweatshirt he was wearing. "Layering – it's the best way to stay warm. You have something outside to break the wind and then tighter clothing close to your body to keep the heat in."

Jessie finished snapping the jacket closed and smiled her thanks.

He nodded briefly. "You'll also stay warmer if you keep moving."

Jessie took his advice and started walking again, but this time they kept pace with each other, the path wide enough for them to walk side by side.

Jessie was the first to break the silence. "You've lent me your jacket, and I don't even know your name."

He gave her that lopsided grin again. "Colin – Colin Hill."

"And my name is Jessie Rodriguez," she returned, smiling up at him.

They both turned away at the same instant. Jessie fixed her eyes on the pathway, but her mind was filled with a jumble of confused thoughts and feelings. The last thing she needed was to be getting interested in another guy. As if she didn't have enough problems already.

"There you are!"

Jessie saw David striding toward them.

"Hey," she said in greeting, happy as always to see the big brother she adored. He reminded her of Zorro, the swashbuckling hero who was always ready to rescue her from any scrape she got into. But she didn't need rescuing now. And she didn't like the frown on his face or the way his dark eyes were clouded with concern; she was fine.

"Where ya been?" David demanded, "I was about ready to send out a posse for you."

Jessie rolled her eyes. Was everyone up here going to treat her like a child? "I was just out for a walk."

David was eyeing Colin now as he said, "It's a little late to be out walking, isn't it?"

Colin's face hardened into a mask before he spun around and walked away from them.

"Wait!" Jessie called.

Colin paused to look back at her, his face expressionless.

"Thanks," Jessie said.

Colin's eyes softened a little but he didn't smile or say a word. Jessie watched him until he became lost in the shadows.

Turning to go, she realized David was staring at her.

"What?" she demanded.

His face relaxed into his trademark grin. He shook his head. "I guess I just have to get used to you growing up. Last time I saw you, you were –"

"Fourteen years old with pigtails and braces," Jessie finished for him.

"Yeah." David grinned. "And now, you're a beautiful young lady with all these guys hanging around."

Jessie laughed. "Guy – not guys," she corrected as they began to walk again. "Actually," her smile faded, "I don't seem to be too popular around here."

David threw her a questioning glance.

"My accent, my music, my clothes – everything!" Jessie exclaimed with a tinge of bitterness in her voice.

The lights from the lodge illuminated David's face as he stopped to briefly assess her. "Corrie might have something you could borrow," he suggested.

Jessie threw up her hands and gave a cry of exasperation. Ignoring David's calls, she ran the rest of the way to the lodge. Flinging open the door, she walked quickly through the dining hall then ran up the spiral staircase to the bedroom she was sharing with David's fiancée.

Jessie tore off Colin's jacket and flung it across the room, then took off the expensive cardigan and stuffed it into the bottom of her tote bag.

A sound at the door caused Jessie to spin around, ready to lash out at whoever was there. All the fire went out of her when she saw that it was Coralee. It was one thing to get mad at your brother – quite another to blow up at your brother's fiancée, especially when you'd just met her that day.

"Jessie, are you all right, honey?"

Coralee sounded genuinely concerned. Jessie smiled reassuringly at her. "I'm fine."

Coralee was pretty – pretty enough to be a fashion model – and living so far north hadn't affected her ability to dress in style. She was looking good now in a pair of lime silk shantung pants and a classic white button-down shirt. Her ebony curls were tied back with a silk scarf, and she wore large, thin gold hoop earrings. Her lipstick and eyeliner looked freshly applied.

Her future sister-in-law was gazing as intently at Jessie as she was at her – but Coralee wasn't thinking about clothes or makeup.

"I'm here for you," she said gently. "If you ever need to talk…"

"I'm fine!" Jessie spoke emphatically. What was wrong with everyone here? If they weren't treating her like a four-year-old, they were acting as if she were a mental patient!

Coralee turned to go then spied the discarded jacket lying on the floor. "Isn't this Colin's?" she asked, stooping to pick it up.

"Yeah, so what? I was cold; he lent me his jacket. No big deal."

Coralee folded it loosely and laid it over a chair. Her hand lingered on the jacket for a moment as she said, "Jessie, I'm gonna be your sister-in-law." She paused. "I'd also like to be your friend."

Jessie gave her a half-hearted smile and turned away.

When she heard the door close, she flopped down on the bed with a sigh.

Jessie was staring absently at the slopping ceiling and skylight when another knock sounded on the door.

It was Coralee again. "I brought you a cup of hot chocolate."

Jessie raised herself to a sitting position and mustered a smile as she took the proffered cup. "Thanks," she said, and took a sip.

"If you'd like to come down for a while…"

Jessie shook her head. "I'm kinda tired."

Coralee smiled understandingly. "You put on a lot of miles today." She reached over and touched Jessie's arm. "Thank you for coming all that way for our wedding."

She headed toward the door but turned back with her hand on the doorknob. "I'm really glad you're here, Jess."

Her voice held such sincerity that Jessie felt obliged to smile in response.

She actually was quite tired and was already in bed when Coralee came back into the room carrying her sleeping baby. She gently laid him in the crib beside her bed and kissed him. Then she stood for a moment longer just looking down at him in the dimly lit room before she turned and noticed Jessie watching her.

"You're still awake," Coralee whispered as she moved toward her bed and kicked off her shoes.

Jessie smiled faintly. Something had been puzzling her. She knew that David was staying in one of the cabins on the property. "Coralee," she began in a hesitant voice, "why do you sleep up here?"

Coralee furrowed her brow and lifted her shoulders slightly. "This is my room, Jess."

Jessie hesitated unsure how to continue. "What I mean is, why aren't you sleeping with David?"

Coralee sank onto her bed and stared at Jessie, her eyes open wide with astonishment. "We're not married yet," she said in a whisper.

Jessie groaned and rolled her eyes. How could anyone who looked so rad be at the same time so incredibly naive? "You already have a baby."

Coralee leaned forward and gently explained. "Michael is our foster son, Jessie. We've already got the paper work started – and after our wedding, David and I are going to legally adopt him."

Jessie was silent a moment before speaking again. "You mean you and David haven't even…"

Coralee smiled. "David and I love each other – a lot," she said softly. "It will be worth the wait."

"But don't you think you should try it out first?" Jessie asked, wrinkling her nose. "What if – I don't know…"

Coralee interrupted with bubbling, joyous laughter. "I think, when the time comes, we won't need a rehearsal." Her eyes twinkled merrily. "People have been doin' it since Adam and Eve."

Jessie turned away.

"Hey, girl." Coralee's gentle voice drew her back. "I didn't mean to make light of your concerns."

Jessie smiled wearily. "It's okay. I just didn't know about Michael and all."

"I'm surprised David didn't tell you."

Jessie shrugged. "He told me lots about Michael. I just assumed from the way he was talking that you were the birth parents. He…" Jessie hesitated. "He looks a bit like you."

Coralee laughed. "You mean African-American?"

Jessie felt her face grow red. "Yeah, but not as dark."

Coralee smiled graciously. "We could be his biological parents, but we're not." She shook her head sadly. "We'll never know who they were. No records were kept on those babies."

Jessie sat upright. "What do you mean *those babies*? I thought there was always a record kept – at least of the birth mother."

Coralee looked puzzled. "Jess, didn't David tell you what he's been doing up here all these years?"

Jessie shook her head. "He said he'd tell me when I got here."

Coralee paused thoughtfully. "Maybe he wants to tell you himself."

"No, tell me now."

Coralee drew her long legs up onto the bed and grabbed a couple of pillows to settle into a more comfortable position before continuing. "We're an international organization called "Rachel's Children." Up until last fall, we were operating secretly here at Goldrock Lodge and on the rest of the old mine property surrounding it."

Jessie listened intently. She'd known that her brother was involved with some kind of undercover work – it had actually been kind of fun for Jessie to get the encoded emails that let them know that David was alive and well, even if he hadn't been able to reveal his location.

"He said that he's been working as a doctor."

"Yes," Coralee confirmed. "Under the mentoring of Doctor Donovan Ryley, David has become an excellent neonatal surgeon." Her voice softened. "He was on the team that saved Michael."

"Saved him?"

"Michael was one of our youngest – born at just twenty-one weeks." Coralee shook her head. "We almost lost him twice."

"I think there's somethin' I'm missing here." Jessie frowned. "And you haven't told me why there's no record of his birth mother."

Coralee nodded slowly. "I'm just surprised that you haven't heard about our work. With all the reporters we had here last fall, I thought for sure the whole world knew. And David didn't tell you?"

"He probably thought I'm too young to understand!"

"Yes," Coralee said with a nod. "Sometimes, when we haven't seen someone for a long time, in our minds, they sort of stay the age that we remember them. That's probably what happened between you and David."

"You got that right!" Jessie exclaimed. "He treats me like I'm ten years old!"

"I'm sure that'll change," Coralee reassured her.

"You were going to tell me about Michael," Jessie prompted.

"Yes." Coralee's eyes grew sad. "You've probably heard of the use of fetal tissue for research and even the transplant of organs or tissues," her voice hardened, "into those considered more worthy of life."

Jessie could only nod.

Coralee wasn't looking at her now. She had turned her head to face the sleeping child. "We don't know who Michael's parents are because he was just one of several experimental embryos that survived to be implanted into a surrogate womb. In some of the earlier cases, the surrogate mother's egg was used, but in Michael's case, both the egg and sperm were anonymous donations."

"But…"

Coralee's eyes were brimming with tears as she turned back toward Jessie. "It's the epitome of rebellion against the Creator. Where He intended life, they had purposely planned for death." The tears overflowed and spilled down her cheeks. "To them, Michael was just a spare-parts department."

Jessie looked over at the sleeping baby.

A sliver of moonlight caressed his face, illuminating the soft eyelashes, little button nose and gently curved lips.

"I'm sorry," Coralee said, reaching for a tissue. "I'm not usually so weepy."

"It's okay."

Coralee smiled affectionately at her. "We should get some sleep."

"Yeah." Jessie sighed, feeling suddenly very tired.

Corrie's cheerful "Goodnight, new little sister" was returned with a mumble as Jessie put her head on the pillow and pulled the blankets up over her shoulders.

Coralee too settled down under the covers, her face turned toward little baby Michael asleep in the crib.

Chapter Two

Morning seemed to come all too soon for Jessie. Coralee was definitely a morning person – or maybe she was just excited about her upcoming wedding. Her cheery greeting grated harshly on Jessie's ears.

"Hey, girl! You gonna sleep all day or what?"

Jessie groaned and put a pillow over her head, but Coralee just laughed and pulled it away.

"C'mon Jess – we got a wedding to get ready for!"

Jessie flung the covers back and sat up. "What do you need me for? I'm not the one getting married."

Coralee shook her head and, with an affectionate grin, began to tick off the items on her fingers as she spoke. "You gotta try on your dress, decide how you want to wear your hair, meet the other bridesmaids…"

"Okay, okay," Jessie protested. "I'm getting up. Just give me a minute."

"Would you like a glass of orange juice or something?"

Jessie nodded and struggled out of bed. Time to face another day.

When Coralee returned a few minutes later, Jessie wasn't much further along. She still had her nightshirt on, and clothes were scattered over both beds and a couple of chairs.

"Having a rummage sale?" Coralee quipped.

Jessie dropped into a chair and surveyed the mess.

"Hey, you look like you just lost your best friend."

As a matter of fact, I did lose my best friend. At least, I thought he was my best friend…

Coralee handed her the orange juice and remained bent over her for a moment. "What's bothering you, hon?"

Jessie shrugged and turned away.

"I would like you to meet the other bridesmaids," Coralee said gently.

"I don't have anything to wear," Jessie said dejectedly.

"You what?" Coralee's voice rose in surprise. "Girl, what're you talkin' 'bout? Your clothes are awesome!"

Jessie watched as Coralee looked through her stuff and picked out an ivory turtleneck sweater. "This would look great with those pants you were wearing last night."

Jessie smiled faintly and took the clothes from Coralee.

"Somethin' else bothering you, Jess?"

Nothing you can fix.

"No," Jessie said aloud. "I'm fine."

"Well," Coralee said, "I guess I'll see you downstairs then."

Jessie nodded and turned to look for her brown tweeds.

They were all gathered around the fireplace at the south end of the lodge when she arrived downstairs some moments later. Jessie walked past the tables and chairs in the large dining hall on her right, and the open doorway of the kitchen on her left, before coming to a halt near the base of the second spiral staircase that also led to the upstairs bedrooms. Jessie pasted a smile on her face and tried to make her voice sound cheerful. "Good morning!"

"Hey, kiddo," David said as he rose to greet her. Coralee stood with him and together they ushered Jessie toward the others.

"This is Jamie and her daughter Rosalee," David said, introducing a pretty young woman with long black hair and delicately chiseled features. Jamie was holding a chubby baby girl and was wearing a T-shirt with a picture of a stork on it, proudly proclaiming that she was expecting another child.

"July eighth," Jamie answered Jessie's unspoken question.

"And this is Jenny, our other bridesmaid, and her daughter Missy." Coralee smiled in the direction of a woman with curly auburn hair. A little girl who looked about four years old was sitting on the couch beside her, listening to a CD and moving her fingers across the page of a book on her lap.

As Jessie came closer, she realized that the little girl with the beautiful dark curls must be visually impaired; the book she was "reading" was in Braille.

Martha Peters, Coralee's mother, arrived at that moment with a plateful of muffins and a pot of coffee. David helped himself to a muffin and kissed Coralee goodbye, saying he was heading over to visit Jeff, his best man.

It seemed strange to see David kissing someone. For just a moment, Jessie felt the tiniest twinge of jealousy. But as he passed by, David had a wink and a smile just for her. "You're not losing a brother; you're gaining a sister," he whispered close to her ear. Jessie couldn't help smiling in return.

Tom Peters was coming toward the group as David was leaving. The older man had baby Michael in his arms. They'd obviously been out for a walk together; their cheeks were ruddy from the cold. David paused to kiss the baby and greet him. "Hey, little man."

"Just going over to Jeff's for a while," David repeated for Tom's benefit, then began to whistle a little tune as he headed toward the door.

Coralee took the baby from her father's arms and her voice took on a higher pitch as she asked her young son,

"Did you have a nice walk with Grandpa?" Michael made little baby sounds and wiggled contentedly in her arms.

The love in her eyes was so obvious that everyone around her was smiling too. As Coralee took off his snowsuit, Jenny commented on how big he was growing and how healthy he looked.

"Soon he'll be as big as Rosie here," Jamie said with a smile.

"They're the same age," Coralee told Jessie, "but Michael got off to a slower start." She beamed fondly down at him again. "He's catching up though, aren't you, Mikey?"

The conversation seemed to naturally center on babies, and Jessie valiantly tried to focus as it passed from teething to the various stages of sitting, crawling, and standing.

Martha occasionally interjected grandmotherly advice, but Jessie noticed that Jenny wasn't talking much. It wasn't until the subject shifted to Jamie's pregnancy that Jenny shyly told them that she was expecting as well. Her baby would be born sometime in December.

Exclamations of joy and congratulations filled the room, and Jenny positively glowed.

"Well, at least it won't affect how your dress fits for the wedding," Coralee said. "Which reminds me, we should really be working on that."

Jamie propped her baby in the corner of the sofa, went to a nearby dining table and lifted a shimmering chiffon gown for them to see. The lavender dress had wide straps, a high waist and soft flowing lines that fell to the floor. Jamie held it up close to Jessie. "It looks like a pretty good fit. We did them according to the measurements you sent us." She laughed. "As long as you're not pregnant, too…"

Jessie's heart raced. The images in the room lost their edge, the scene shifting into a confused blur of movement. Laughter seemed to rise in waves around her, huge walls of water threatening to engulf her.

Jessie backed away until she found herself up against a wall then looked around for a way of escape. There was a hallway to her left that seemed to lead to an outside door. There were coats hanging on the walls.

As Jessie headed toward the door, she heard Coralee call, "Hey, where ya goin'?"

Jessie pulled open the first door and reached for the handle of the second one. Coralee's voice pursued her. "What about the dress?"

Jessie pulled open the second door and breathed in the sharp cold air.

"Jessie!"

Her breath was coming in short gasps as she called back, "I'll try it on later. I don't feel good. I need some air."

Jessie started to run. She saw the lake, dark and forbidding, and it drew her like a magnet.

Out on the dock, Jessie slowed to a walk and finally stood at the end. There were no houses in sight and it seemed, looking out across the frozen expanse, that there was no one else in the universe – just endless ice and trees and sky. Dark clouds hung low, threatening snow or freezing rain. Jessie shivered in the cold wind and wished she had thought to grab a coat.

"It's a little cold for swimming."

The voice startled her. Jessie spun around to see Colin sauntering down the dock toward her.

"And," he continued with a grin, "it's definitely too cold to be standing out here without a jacket on."

Jessie turned away. She was in no mood to be laughed at again.

But his voice was gentler now as he held out his jacket for her. "You can put this on if you want."

Jessie slipped her arms through the sleeves and zipped up the warm parka. She glanced up at him shyly. "Thanks – again."

"We'd be more out of the wind if we sat down."

Jessie smiled faintly and joined Colin as he bent his long legs to sit at the end of the dock. Jessie let her legs dangle over the edge, her feet barely skimming the hard surface of the ice.

The minutes passed with neither of them speaking. Jessie marveled at Colin's ability to sense her mood and not fill the silence with meaningless chatter. She began to relax a little and her normally good-humored personality resurfaced. She turned toward Colin with a broad smile. "How'd you know I was out here, needing another coat? You some kind of superhero who goes around with an endless supply of jackets looking to rescue fair maidens in distress?"

Colin laughed. "I don't have an endless supply; that's my last one. And I was heading down here anyway. Mr. Peters wanted me to check on the life buoys. With the children playing outside and the ice getting thinner..." Colin left the sentence unfinished, the meaning clear.

"Do you work for him – or is this another of your good deeds?" Jessie quipped.

Colin lifted an eyebrow and grinned. "I'm an employee of Mr. Peters."

"What do you do?" Jessie asked, curious now.

Colin smiled. "Just about everything – from shoveling snow in the winter to cleaning fish in the summer. Sometimes I do a little guiding and general maintenance on the boats." He nodded in Jessie's direction. "We don't usually have many guests at the lodge in the winter."

They both looked out toward the frozen lake again. A little patch of blue was breaking through the dark cloud cover. Maybe they wouldn't have snow after all.

"It'll be breakup soon," Colin spoke into the silence.

Jessie turned toward him. "Does that mean the ice isn't safe to walk on anymore?"

"Yeah, it's pretty unstable right now."

Jessie tapped her shoe. "It feels solid enough here."

Colin shook his head. "It's really deceptive."

Jessie waited for him to continue.

"You see," he began, "when it's a sunny day, some of the ice on the surface melts and forms a layer of water that sits on top of the ice. But some of that water seeps down into air pockets in the one or two feet of ice that's left at this time of the year."

Colin paused and waited for her to nod before continuing. "It forms what's called 'candle ice.' It hangs down like candles into the water, but perhaps a better name would be 'stalactite ice' because the pieces are jagged and irregular like stalactites. The shards of ice are actually sharp enough to cut through the skin if you had to break up the ice around, for example, a deer that had fallen in. This lake," he swept his hand in a semi-circle, "may look solid enough but it's really quite fragile – and dangerous."

Jessie gazed with fascination at the wide expanse of frozen lake. "How much force would it take?" she asked, tapping the ice with her foot again.

"Well, it really depends on how the weight is distributed. Moose and deer are especially vulnerable because so much of their weight is concentrated on the relatively small surface area of the hoof –"

But Jessie wasn't interested in animals. "Would I break through if I jumped on it?"

Colin looked intently at her for a moment before answering. "In some spots, you might break the ice just by walking. Other spots, you might need to jump to break it. It depends on underwater currents or if there's a weakness in the ice for some other reason."

"And would you just bob up again in the same spot?"

"Usually," Colin said slowly. "It depends on what you're wearing. Most people fall through during the winter and have parkas and winter boots on. The soles of winter boots tend to be lighter, and of course a parka will float." He paused before continuing. "You usually just have that one chance though. I've never seen anyone come up to the surface more than once. If they can't get out by themselves or get help, their clothes will get soaked and their body become numb and even if they did have the strength to resurface, it would be hard for them to find the exact spot again where they'd fallen through."

"But I could just break through at the new spot."

Colin shook his head. "No. You see, the reason you would break through while walking – or jumping..." He hesitated, a frown of consternation on his face. "The reason is that you are putting a lot of weight on a relatively small surface area – like the moose or deer. But if you were under the ice, the water would make you virtually weightless and the only pressure that you could exert would be maybe five or ten pounds – just what you could press up with your hands."

Jessie listened intently as Colin continued, "You wouldn't have a lot of strength though because of the effect of the cold water on your muscles. And it's dark down there and you would be suffering from hypothermia – "

"Hypothermia – how soon?"

"I don't know." Colin's voice had a slight edge to it now. "What do you want to know all this stuff for?"

"I'm just curious!" Jessie said defensively. "You think I'm planning a murder or something?"

Colin swallowed hard and turned away.

What had she said?

"I'm sorry."

Colin shook his head but didn't look at her. His voice, when he spoke, was low and sad. "My uncle passed away suddenly just a few months ago – on the first of September. And then just a few weeks after that, a woman who was my foster mom for two years, she – uh, she was killed."

Jessie waited for him to continue.

"It's still in the court system." He lifted his eyes slowly to face her. "I think they're going for manslaughter."

Jessie reached out a hand and touched his knee, wishing she could comfort him somehow. "I'm so sorry," she said.

Colin smiled faintly and lifted a shoulder in a half-hearted shrug.

"So you're not going to push me off the dock?" Colin quipped in an obvious attempt to lighten the conversation.

"Not today," Jessie responded in kind.

Colin's face grew serious again. "I've been through the ice a couple of times myself. It can be kind of tricky to get out because the ice around the hole gets covered with water, making it even more slippery. It's hard to get a grip on anything to pull yourself out with. And you don't really have that much time," he added, "before your hands are too numb to be of any use."

"How much time?" Jessie asked.

Colin looked questioningly at her.

"How long before you can't move? And do you just sink under the water then and drown – or would you freeze to death first?"

"I don't know," Colin admitted. "I've known people that have been under the water for a long time and lived to tell about it. And I've known about people who have fallen through the ice…" he lowered his voice to almost a whisper "…and they haven't survived."

"Jessica Elvira Rodriguez!" The stern voice forestalled any further conversation.

Jessie groaned and stole a look at Colin.

"Elvira?" he mouthed, one eyelid shooting up as he grinned broadly.

But her brother was upon them now. Jessica couldn't ever remember him being angry with her before – but he was sure smokin' now!

"What's going on with you?" he demanded. "You're sitting here having a nice little conversation with," he paused and looked meaningfully at Colin, "someone who's getting paid by the hour."

Colin stood silently to his feet and walked away as David continued his tirade. "Meanwhile, I come back to find Corrie crying. She seems to think that she offended you somehow."

Jessie's eyes were following Colin as he departed, but her thoughts were on the ladies at the lodge and what they'd been talking about.

But David couldn't read her mind, and he misinterpreted her fixed gaze.

"When did you become so boy-crazy Jess? I don't remember –"

Sadness flared into anger. Jessie jumped to her feet. "You don't know anything about me – not one single thing!"

Chapter Three

"Jess, wait!"

She slowed from running into a fast walk but didn't look up as her brother came alongside.

"I just want to know what Corrie said or did to upset you so much," David said in a voice more sympathetic than angry now.

Jessie and David had no other brothers or sisters, and the wide age difference had only strengthened the bond between the two of them. After their dad had left, David had taken on almost a fatherly role in her life, helping her with school projects, going to her sports events, and giving sometimes more advice than she wanted or needed. When he'd suddenly disappeared out of her life, Jessie had been devastated. His brief emails had been her lifeline, but there had been a lot that he couldn't – or wouldn't – tell her. And he hadn't been there when she'd needed him most.

"I'd like my two favorite women to get along with each other."

Something in the way he said it made Jessie stop. She looked up, her eyes meeting his. "I'll try harder," she said.

David's face was still etched with concern. "Don't you like Corrie?"

Jessie put her hands up in protest. "No, man – she's cool." Jessie paused, trying to think of some compliment. "She's got some awesome clothes."

David's face broke into a massive grin and he threw back his head and laughed. "Well, I guess that's something," he said, still shaking his head as they began to walk again. "Awesome clothes, huh?"

Jessie smiled. It was good to hear David laughing. It was the thing she'd missed the most after he'd left.

"I think she wants me to try on a dress," Jessie said as they approached the door of the lodge.

David shook his head. "Not right now. Martha sent me to tell you that lunch is ready."

They stepped into the dining hall, which looked cavernous and gloomy without the benefit of the sun coming through the cathedral-size windows and numerous skylights. The chandeliers hanging high above them were turned on but didn't help to dispel the gray afternoon light.

"I think we're in for a storm." Tom's voice carried from across the hall.

But it was Martha who was bustling toward them. "There you are!"

"She was just down by the dock," David explained.

The older woman smiled inquiringly at Jessie. "How're you doing, hon?"

Jessie nodded and attempted a smile in return.

Martha took her arm and led her to where several of the small, rough-hewn and varnished dining tables had been pushed together to make a larger one. "Colin's grandpa sent over a big pot of moose stew for us," she said, showing Jessie to a chair between her husband and Colin.

Tom nodded and smiled in her direction, and Jessie returned the greeting before turning to Colin. "Sorry I got you into trouble with David," she whispered.

Colin shrugged. "He ain't my boss."

"Who ain't your boss?" Tom demanded.

"Someone who thought he was," Colin replied diplomatically.

Jessie glanced down the length of the table at David, but he was deep in conversation with Coralee and didn't seem aware of anyone else.

Martha arrived with a large plate of tea biscuits just then and asked Tom if he would carry in the pot of stew.

Colin turned to Jessie. "Grandpa Pipe makes really good moose stew."

Jessie had to laugh. "Grandpa Pipe?"

Colin grinned. "I don't even think about his name anymore. He's been Grandpa Pipe to me since I was old enough to talk, but I suppose it's because he usually has a pipe in his mouth and one or two more in his shirt pocket. There's always a few more lying here and there around the cabin, too."

The stew arrived and it looked and smelled delicious!

Suddenly everyone was joining hands. Jessie looked awkwardly around the table as those present silently bowed their heads. Tom cleared his throat and began to talk to God as if He were right there in the room with them! It seemed strange coming from the lips of this almost seven-foot-tall giant of a man with the booming voice and authoritative manner. He called God "precious Lord Jesus" and not only thanked Him for the food but prayed for each person around the table! Jessie stiffened with apprehension as her turn came but Tom simply asked for "Your hand of mercy to be upon our special guest, Jessie," and added, "We thank You that she is here with us today." He closed the prayer with the words, "Thy kingdom come; Thy will be done. We love You, Jesus. Amen."

The "amen" was echoed around the table as the clinking of silverware and lively chatter began. Food was passed and Jessie soon found her plate filled with thick moose stew and a hot buttered biscuit.

"Do you know everyone here?" Colin asked after a moment.

Jessie looked around. She recognized all of them except for one. "The man on the other side of Missy. He's cutting her piece of stew meat into smaller bites, and talking to her."

"That's her dad. His name is Jeff Peters," Colin answered.

"My son," Tom put in.

Jessie tried to be surreptitious as she glanced from Jeff, who was quite obviously Caucasian, and then back to Tom, who was just as obviously African-American, as were his wife and daughter.

But the older man had seen her and was chuckling in a deep throaty voice. "Jeff's my adopted son," he clarified.

"Oh, of course," Jessie quickly recovered her composure. Why hadn't she thought of that? But then the little girl, Missy, must have been, in turn, adopted, since Jeff and his wife were both white, and the little girl had the coloring and features of an African-American child. Was everyone in this place adopted?

As if in answer to her unspoken question, Tom introduced the other child sitting at the table. "Bobby is also one of our chosen children." This Jessie would not have guessed, since his coloring was similar to that of his adoptive parents.

"He has Down syndrome," Tom said in a lowered voice, but he needn't have worried. Bobby and Missy had finished their meal, and Bobby was asking Martha for permission for both of them to leave the table and try out the new computer program that someone named Charles had designed for him. Jessie remembered hearing that name mentioned before. Oh, yes, he was the one who had designed the lodge. That must have taken some engineering, building the two-story, split-level log frame up against a solid rock face.

After the children had left the table, Jenny, sitting adjacent to Jessie, commented, "Charles is really getting into computer programming now that he's not busy helping us forge birth certificates and contacting prospective parents on the Internet."

"*Forging birth certificates?*" Jessie asked incredulously.

"You haven't told her?" Martha directed the question to David.

"I've told her a bit," Coralee quickly put in.

Jessie looked at the faces around the table, now all turned in her direction.

Tom spoke first. "We were up against a very powerful organization called FORT, which stands for Fetal Organ Retrieval Technologies." His voice grew quieter, and there was a hush around the table as he continued. "They used aborted fetuses or produced their own to be sold to various markets. The organs and tissue were mostly sold to researchers, but some were used for organ transplant. Whole babies were often sent to university science labs to replace animal specimens."

"We raided FORT on several occasions." David continued the story. "We rescued as many babies as we could."

"But if they were aborted," Jessie broke in, "they'd be dead."

"In a sense, they weren't truly aborted," David responded. "The babies were sedated while still inside the womb and kept in that state even after being transferred to the special 'units' that they were stored in. This kept the tissues and organs still functioning and 'fresh' so to speak. Only a few of the babies were full term, and they were usually 'special orders.' There was a high cost involved with those." David paused and glanced up at Jenny briefly before continuing. "Most of the babies were premature and, depending on how many organs had already been harvested from them, they would have more or less of a chance of survival."

"So," Jessie looked around accusingly, "you all stole those babies."

"We prefer the term 'rescue,'" Martha said gently.

"I can see that in a case like Michael's." Jessie nodded in Coralee's direction. "But what about if a woman chose to terminate her pregnancy? What right do you have to bring that baby into the world – and forge papers – and adopt..." Jessie's voice had risen as she spoke and now trembled a little as she continued. "You're as much in the black market baby business as that – what did you call it – FORT? You're just like them!"

She could see it in their eyes. She'd alienated every one of them. Jessie stood quickly to her feet. Maybe she should just head back home again. This whole thing was just going from bad to worse. Coralee already had two bridesmaids.

"Jessie!"

She heard someone behind her on the stairs. Jessie turned back as they reached the landing. It was Jenny.

Jenny looked ready to cry, and her voice shook a little as she asked, "Could I talk with you for a moment, Jessie?"

Everything in Jess recoiled against it. But there was something in the gentle appeal that she found impossible to refuse. She glanced down over the railing to the group at the table. Every eye was on her and Jenny.

"I guess," she finally answered, hurrying to her bedroom.

Jenny followed her inside and quietly shut the door.

Jessie flopped down on the bed, crossed her arms and looked defiantly up at the woman. "So?"

Jenny took a deep breath as if to compose herself. She walked slowly over to Coralee's bed and sat down. "My daughter, Missy..." she began.

Jessie rolled her eyes – another sob story like Coralee and Michael's. "I know, I know. You feel like some hero for *rescuing* her – but my question is What about the woman who should have had the right to terminate her pregnancy? Where do her feelings come into this?"

Jenny swallowed hard and looked closer to tears than ever. "I am that woman."

Jessie shook her head in annoyance. "I don't mean her adoptive mother. I mean the woman who –"

Jenny interrupted her, no longer able to hold back the tears spilling down her cheeks. "I am Missy's birth mother."

Jessie sat up slowly, allowing herself time to digest the information.

She didn't meet Jenny's eyes even as she spoke. "I'm sorry."

"Nothing to be sorry about," came the gentle reply. "Every day I thank the Lord for returning my precious baby girl to me."

Jessie looked up. "But you had chosen…"

Jenny shook her head. "I had no idea what I was doing. I was lonely and afraid and I didn't know – I didn't know how much it would hurt – and keep on hurting." She smiled sadly at Jessie. "Missy was three years old before I knew that she was alive. I can't begin to describe the guilt and anguish I went through in those three years."

Jessie was silent a moment before asking, "Did you know that she was blind. Is that why you were going to –"

But Jenny was shaking her head. "She had gorgeous brown eyes. I wasn't supposed to see her – but I did."

Jessie waited silently for her to continue.

"Then FORT took those gorgeous eyes and sold them," Jenny finished in a whisper.

There was nothing more to be said. Jessie sat with her head bowed.

She felt a hand lightly touching her knee and looked up into eyes that were filled with concern. "You seem to have especially strong views on this subject," Jenny said. "Do you know someone who is struggling with this kind of a choice?"

Jessie turned away. "Yeah." She had tried to keep her tone casual, but her voice broke and the word came out sounding like a cry for help.

"Would you like to talk about it, Jessie?"

No!

She had already talked to the only other person who mattered.

"No, but thanks for the offer," she replied curtly. Jenny took the hint and left.

Jessie lay back down on the bed, buried her face in her pillow and wept. But it was only a matter of minutes before someone else was knocking on the bedroom door. Jessie swiped at the tears and sat upright again. Why couldn't she have a room with a lock on the door? Why couldn't everyone just leave her alone?

It was Coralee, looking apologetic for interrupting. "Colin was wondering about his coat. Actually," Coralee looked puzzled, "he says you have both of his jackets."

"The other one's downstairs." Jessie strode over and grabbed the wool and leather jacket that Colin had lent her the night before and held it out to Coralee.

"He, uh, wondered if you might like to go for a walk."

A walk. A chance to get away from this place!

"You can go down through the back way if you like."

Jessie quickly put on a pair of flat-heeled shoes and slipped her beige trench coat over the turtleneck sweater she was wearing. This time she'd be properly dressed for walking!

Jessie thought Coralee was going to lead her down the spiral staircase at the south end of the building and out the side door where she had gone earlier that day. Instead she led her north along the gallery and into the furthest of the three upstairs bedrooms. Bewildered, Jessie followed as

Coralee went into a large walk-in closet. Jessie was even more surprised when Coralee pushed aside some hanging clothes to reveal a hidden door.

Coralee flashed a smile. "This was part of our secret entrance to our underground operations during our Rachel's Children days."

Beyond the door was a set of stairs. Jessie followed Coralee down the steps, which led to another door that opened into a garage. Coralee waved toward a door in the adjacent wall. "That leads outside."

"Thanks," Jessie said sincerely.

Colin was waiting for her around the front of the building.

"Your other one's inside," Jessie said as she handed him his jacket.

His friendly smile put Jessie immediately at ease.

She noticed that Colin had the empty stew pot in one hand. He put on his jacket then led Jessie along the front of the lodge and then further north toward the path they'd been on the previous night.

Jessie fell into step beside him, once more thankful that Colin didn't feel the need to talk just to fill the silences. It was so relaxing to be with him, walking on the tree-lined pathway, enjoying the natural sounds around her. The wind made a whistling sound through the trees; a raven cawed from far overhead; and somewhere a dog barked.

They had been walking only a short time when they heard a rhythmic drumming sound. Colin put his arm on hers to stop her and signaled for silence. He looked around in the trees then pointed and whispered, "Pileated woodpecker."

Not more than fifteen feet away, a large black bird with white neck stripes and a prominent red crest was using its powerful bill to drill into the trunk of a tree.

"That's a male," Colin said softly. "See the red mustache."

Jessie laughed and the bird immediately took flight with a flash of white underwings and a laugh of it's own that sounded like *kik-kik-kik-kik.*

They watched until it soared out of sight before continuing on their way.

Jessie shook her head and chuckled. "Red mustache, huh?"

"It's true!" Colin protested.

"Mm-hmm."

Chapter Four

Jessie and Colin turned off the main path and walked down a smaller one until it ended in a clearing with a log cabin built on a hill overlooking the lake.

There was a small square window on their right as Colin led the way up the two steps and put his hand on the old-fashioned black metal latch of the wooden door.

As Jessie stepped into the cabin, she felt suddenly transported back in time.

There was a bed on either side, the frames made of rough lumber and each covered with a mattress, bare now except for a pile of blankets and a single pillow on each.

Straight ahead, in the middle of the cabin, two stoves were connected with elbows to a single pipe that went up into the roof. The stove facing west toward the lake was a cast-iron cookstove, and the other, a pot-bellied one, seemed to be primarily for heat, although a metal pan with water sat on it.

Colin hung his coat on one of several wooden pegs that protruded from the walls on either side of them. He took Jessie's coat and hung it up as well. There were no pictures on the walls, but beyond a small window on Jessie's left a gun rack with three long guns hung on the wall above the bed. Her eyes were drawn further down toward the larger window facing the lake and the small table covered with a brightly flowered oilcloth and surrounded by three arrowback chairs.

The entire cabin looked to be only slightly larger than her bedroom back home. "How many people live here?" Jessie whispered, awestruck.

Colin grinned. "Just my grandfather and me now. After my parents passed away and he took us kids in, there were three and sometimes four of us here."

Jessie took a step forward and only then noticed that they were not alone. A gray-haired man with weathered and wrinkled skin was sitting on a chair puffing contentedly on his pipe. He had been partially hidden from her view by the woodstoves. Beyond him, in the far northeastern corner, Jessie could see another bed and an old oak dresser.

"My grandfather," Colin said, leading her toward him.

Jessie was embarrassed to realize that he'd been there the whole time she'd been gawking around the cabin, but as she approached the old man, Jessie saw only an amused grin and a sparkle in his eye.

Colin introduced her, or at least that's what Jessie assumed because she heard both her name and her brother's amidst the other unrecognizable words.

"*Boozhoo*," the older man greeted her.

Jessie hesitated. "I don't speak your language," she whispered to Colin.

"That's okay," he reassured her. "I'll translate."

Colin put the stew pot on a lower shelf of the cupboards that lined the walls of the northwest corner of the cabin, and exchanged some more words with his grandfather while Jessie remained where she was, feeling more out of place by the moment.

It got a little easier after she and Colin were seated at the table and served tea by his grandfather. It was a strong dark brew that he poured from an enamel teapot that had been sitting at the back of the cookstove. Upon Colin's recommendation, Jessie added a couple of spoonfuls of sugar and some of the canned evaporated milk. She took a sip and was surprised to find that it was actually quite good!

Grandpa Pipe laughed, pointed to the teapot and spoke a few words.

"He says that's good strong Indian tea," Colin interpreted, "strong enough to tan a moose hide."

They laughed together and Jessie felt the last of her apprehensions melt away. The conversation flowed spontaneously after that. Colin was a good interpreter, maintaining the tone and intent of the speaker as he shifted quickly from one language to another.

Colin described for Pipe their sighting of a pileated woodpecker. Jessie maintained her disbelief that a male could be distinguished by its mustache, but Pipe told her with a straight face that it was absolutely true.

Colin poured more tea while the older man tapped out the contents of his pipe and carefully refilled and relit it.

"Settling into story mode," Colin informed Jessie with a grin.

Sure enough, Pipe launched into a tale about his younger years, pausing occasionally for Colin to interpret.

"I remember when I was young, we were canoeing past this rock and we could hear some baby birds. We went past that same spot two more times that day and didn't see any mother – just the squawking babies.

"So me and my friend went climbing up this rock. There was a ledge right near the top. I couldn't quite reach it. My friend – he was below me and could guide my hand as I reached around with a stick. I knocked the one bird out of its nest but it didn't have enough feathers and fell down. The other two had enough feathers and flapped down."

"What kind of bird?" Jessie asked.

Colin had obviously heard the story before. "Ravens," he answered without consulting Pipe.

The old man continued his story. "There they were sitting in the front of the canoe just squawking away. We had some worms for fishing and they gobbled those right down – they were really hungry. Then maybe the motion of the canoe rocked them to sleep because pretty soon they're nodding and then their eyes closed. But then," he chuckled, "they started hiccupping and out those worms came."

"Eewh." Jessie couldn't help wrinkling her nose in disgust.

The other two laughed, then Pipe explained, "They were used to their mother chewing their food for them."

Double gross!

Colin grinned at her and continued to translate. "We got them home and they sat squawking on the table. We had some bacon that was really greasy."

Colin paused as Pipe chuckled again before continuing. "Every time they got a piece of bacon, they got a little bit quieter. Pretty soon, they were completely quiet. You see, the grease had coated their throats."

"So what happened to them?" Jessie wanted to know.

"Oh, we had them for a long time," Pipe answered through Colin. "They're really smart birds. We never kept them in a cage or anything.

"The one especially stuck around a long time. He used to nibble on my ear – not so it hurt – just affectionately." The old man laughed as he recalled the bird. "He used to steal my pipe right out of my pocket. We used to have horses back then to haul logs out of the bush, and that bird would hide things up in the hayloft of the barn. One time he took my pipe – it was still smoking – and he headed right for that hayloft!" Pipe chuckled again before exclaiming, "I sure ran fast that day!

"When we'd go blueberry picking," Pipe continued after a brief pause, "that bird would sit on my shoulder and just eye those berries. Finally he'd pick one out of the bucket and then squawk a little until I gave him a handful."

Colin and Jessie exchanged smiles. Jessie thought she would be content to sit all day and listen to his grandfather's stories.

But the raven saga was coming to an end. "He used to fly around with this other bird. You'd see the two of them ravens up there – necking or something. They'd be gone for a day or two and then he'd come back. Finally he just didn't come back one time."

The wind had been picking up as they talked; Jessie heard the windows rattling occasionally, as a sudden gust shook them.

"Grandpa Pipe says he thinks maybe a storm is brewing." Colin stood up. "We should head back soon."

Jessie rose to her feet also. "Tell your grandfather thank you."

But Colin told her she could try that word herself. He pronounced it carefully and Jessie repeated the two syllables, "*Meegwetch*."

Pipe's face crinkled into a broad grin. "*Meegwetch!*" he returned.

Light rain was falling as they stepped outside, and by the time they were on the main path, it was beginning to rain in earnest.

"C'mon!" Colin laughed. "We'd better run!"

The lodge was in view when the heavens opened and rain fell in huge sheets around them. They made a mad dash toward the building and burst through the front door in a shower of raindrops and laughter.

It took a moment for them to notice that several pairs of eyes were fastened on them. Jessie looked at the group assembled around a large piece of paper on one of the tables. They had obviously been discussing something but seemed hesitant now to continue.

Martha broke away from the others and approached them. "We were just talking about the wedding," she said with a smile. "Come and join us."

Jessie hung up her coat and slipped off her shoes before following Martha. Colin walked slower, staying a few feet behind.

There was another uncomfortable silence before David spoke up. "We were just wondering if you still wanted to be a bridesmaid. We – uh – didn't want to put any pressure on you – if you didn't want to, I mean."

"But I do," Jessie protested. "What would make you think that I didn't?"

"Of course she does," Martha said kindly, drawing Jessie closer and showing her a sketch on the paper. "We were wanting you to walk down with Bobby and Missy. Bobby is the ring bearer and Missy is the flower girl, but we thought they might need someone close by."

Jessie nodded. She knew that Bobby had Down syndrome and Missy was blind. "So you all just need me as a glorified babysitter."

"No, no, not at all," Coralee rushed in. "You're an important part of our wedding."

Jessie tamped down her annoyance. Why did it matter anyway if she didn't have a best man to walk beside?

Everyone was staring at her, waiting for her reaction.

"I'm cool with it," Jessie said with a shrug.

"And the dress?" Martha asked gently.

Jessie looked at Coralee. "I am sorry about that – uh – what happened this morning. You want me to try it on now?"

Coralee gave a little sigh of relief. "Yes, I'll just give Jamie a call. She worked night shift last night but should be awake by now."

Night shift. Jessie knew Jamie was a nurse but thought maybe she'd be on maternity leave by now with less than three months to go. Jessie shrugged; none of her business.

The rain was already letting up, and it was only a matter of moments before Jamie arrived. The group around the table dispersed, and the three young women went together up to Coralee's room.

Jessie changed in the bathroom, and when she reappeared moments later wearing the bridesmaid's dress, Coralee and Jamie both showered her with compliments. Jessie had to admit the mauve did look good on her. The empire waists of the dresses had been designed to accommodate Jamie's growing "baby bump" and Jessie was glad that it gave her the extra room she needed as well.

They spent the rest of the afternoon trying different hairstyles. Coralee had a real talent in this area. "You have such beautiful hair, Jess," she exclaimed. "You could wear it up or down – and it would look great."

"Or maybe half and half," Jamie suggested. "Some of it up and the rest hanging down."

Coralee was following through on her suggestions. "With just a bit on each side to frame your face."

Jessie was surprised to find that she was enjoying herself. This is what she'd missed in not having sisters!

When they started talking about how Coralee would wear her hair, Jessie realized that she hadn't seen her bridal gown yet. Coralee opened the mirrored closet doors and carefully removed her wedding dress.

"Oh!" Jessie exclaimed, "Will you put it on?"

Coralee, with a broad smile, quickly complied and was soon standing before them in the sparkling white chiffon gown, inset with lace and pearls.

"Awesome!" Jessie admired her future sister-in-law.

Time passed quickly as they talked about wedding veils, shoes, flowers, and a special cologne that Coralee had purchased on her last trip to the city.

Before they knew it, Martha was calling them for supper.

The meal was uneventful, and afterward they gathered around the fireplace for coffee and desert. David and Coralee sat on the floor between the chair where Jessie was sitting and the couch where several others were seated. David was talking with Jeff about the possibility of the two of them taking further medical training at a hospital back in the States.

Martha brought in a tray with coffee and hot chocolate, and Jenny helped her mother-in-law with the hostess responsibilities by offering cookies to go with the drinks.

David stopped in mid-sentence and expressed surprise when Jessie chose coffee instead of hot chocolate. Jessie rolled her eyes and shook her head. "She is eighteen, David," Coralee reminded him.

He almost spilled his coffee. "Eighteen! When did that happen?"

Jessie stopped being annoyed with him and joined in the laughter.

"We're all of us a little older, buddy," Jeff quipped. "Older, if not wiser."

But David was looking up at Jessie. "I missed your birthday," he said quietly. "It's around this time of the year, isn't it?"

Jessie nodded. "March fifteenth."

David's eyes were sad. "I've missed a lot of your birthdays, Jess."

It was as if it there were just the two of them in the room. "Yes," she replied.

"I've missed a lot of other things too, haven't I?"

Her voice shook a little as she managed the one word again. "Yes."

"I'm here for you now, Jess."

No, you're not! You can't be. I came here hoping you could help me. But now I know that you can't.

Tears were streaming down her cheeks. Jessie set down her coffee cup with a clatter and ran for the door.

A light breeze blew off the frozen lake, cooling her hot cheeks. Jessie was heading toward the water when David's voice stopped her.

"Please wait."

Jessie stopped and glanced back at David, noticing Coralee was with him.

"Jessie," David said hesitantly, "can't we start over again? A lot has happened in the last few years – for both of us. We're not the people we used to be." His voice softened. "But I'll always be your big brother – and you'll always be my little sister."

Coralee put an arm around her, and Jessie didn't push her away.

"Maybe, if you could understand better what I've been doing here," David continued. "I'd like to show you our underground operation. At least what's left of it," he amended. "A lot of the equipment has been moved over to the health center." He smiled proudly. "We have a better neonatal surgical unit here than in many big city hospitals. Jeff has written several articles for medical journals –"

"David," Coralee interjected, "maybe one thing at a time."

"Oh, of course. I – I'll go ask Tom about the underground tour."

He's trying so hard, Jessie thought.

As David hurried back into the lodge, Coralee moved to link her arm with Jessie's. "We could go for a walk down to the lake, if you like."

Jessie walked silently beside her, still too brimful of emotions to speak.

"This is where I was when I first saw your brother," Coralee said dreamily as they paused on the crest of the hill. "He was coming off a plane with my brother, Jeff. They were laughing about something, then David looked up and saw me. He just stood there looking at me for a minute, then nudged Jeff – who was busy unloading the plane – and pointed up at me. They exchanged some words and then he came up here –"

"Love at first sight." Jessie made no attempt to keep the cynicism out of her voice.

Coralee laughed cheerfully. "Actually, I didn't like him at all at first. He was like this 'Don Juan' character out of some nineteen-thirties movie. I thought he was pretentious and shallow, putting on some kind of debonair act for everyone."

Jessie glanced up at her in surprise, but Coralee was looking dreamily out over the lake again. "Then I got to see his more serious side – and I came to appreciate his wonderful sense of humor – and the genuine love he has for people. And he's really a very good doctor –"

"Who is?"

David was coming toward them, dangling a large set of keys on a ring.

"Your fiancée is singing your praises," Jessie quipped.

"Oh, are you now?" David grinned at Coralee and kissed her lightly. Then he jingled the keys, bowed with a grand flourish and proclaimed, "Rodriguez Underground Tours at your service, mademoiselle, and," he lifted an eyebrow toward Coralee, "soon-to-be madame."

Jessie had to smile. She really was happy for her brother.

It was a surprise to be led back into the house and through the kitchen into the garage to begin their tour, although now that she thought about it, Coralee had mentioned that the secret staircase was built to allow access to their underground operations. It was still a shock though when after David keyed a number into a box by the outside door, the entire wall in front of them lifted up to reveal a dark, cold, and damp cavern.

Chapter Five

Jessie had known that the lodge was built up against a large rock outcropping but could never have imagined this secret entrance into the earth itself.

"It goes down into the mine," Coralee told her, walking into the darkness. Jessie was more hesitant, but David ushered her into the cavern with a cheerful, "Your chariot awaits."

A beam of light cut through the darkness, and Jessie could see an old truck with a homemade sort of camper on the back of it. David handed her a hard hat, and Coralee gave her what looked like a big yellow rain jacket. The light was coming from Coralee's headlamp. David showed Jessie how to turn hers on then helped her to put on her jacket, which fastened with metal clasps.

"I don't suppose we need to close this," Coralee said, motioning toward the door.

David shook his head, and as they got into the cab of the truck he explained to Jessie, "Secrecy used to be quite essential when we were in full swing here."

The roar of the truck's engine sounded especially loud as it echoed off the rock walls. David switched on the headlights and Jessie could see a tunnel sloping down into the darkness. "This is what's called a 'decline,'" Coralee explained as they slowly began their descent. "It was used to move large equipment into the mine. The gold, miners, and smaller pieces of equipment were transported in a type of elevator system called a 'hoist.'"

"We'll go back up that way," David put in.

"And end up at the head frame," Coralee added.

"Head frame?"

"It's that really tall structure over by all the other buildings," David explained; "You can see it from the air."

Jessie nodded, a little in awe of everything that was happening.

They continued their descent in silence until David said, "Ahh, here we are."

It didn't look any different to Jessie but David had stopped the truck, and he and Coralee were getting out so Jessie followed.

It seemed as if they were just continuing down the tunnel, only this time on foot, but Jessie soon realized that they were no longer descending but going into a horizontal tunnel.

"This is called a stope," David informed her. "The gold is mined out in sections like this. If you were to look at a cross-section of the mine, it would look something like that ant farm you used to have. Do you remember? It was glass on both sides and you could see the little tunnels that the ants made."

Jessie smiled. She remembered. David had loved science and just naturally expected her to share his enthusiasm. On his frequent trips home from college, he would often bring her something like a microscope or a chemistry set. She must have been about eight or nine when he'd given her the ant farm. Jessie had valued it more for his sake than for any special interest in zoology. And she'd valued the time they had shared together on such projects.

"Well, here we are."

They had arrived at some sort of wooden structure. Jessie looked further and saw that it was a series of rooms. David selected a key and opened the first door. Stepping in, Jessie realized that the room went deep back into the rock and was actually quite large.

"It seems so strange not having the lights on in here," Coralee mused quietly. She walked further into the room, her headlamp sending a single shaft of light ahead of her.

"This used to be the intensive care nursery." David's voice was also hushed as he laid his hand on a dusty plastic container set on a metal cart.

Coralee shone her light on two other rooms built off the larger one. "These were the neonatal surgeries," she said, heading into the nearer one. "I remember when you wheeled Michael out of here, David. You looked so exhausted but you had this look of triumph in your eyes."

"We fought pretty hard for that little guy's life," David replied.

"Three months premature. It was a miracle he even survived."

Jessie stayed rooted to the spot. *Three months premature – six months. Six months…*

How far along are you? The conversation came unbidden to Jessie's memory.

Almost six months.

Why didn't you tell me sooner?

I don't know. I was afraid. I didn't even want to admit it to myself.

"Jessie, are you okay?"

David's voice came from a great distance.

Her eyes slowly focused on the incubator. She'd been staring at it – thinking of a six-month-old fetus being rescued.

"Jessie, honey, there's a stool right under you. That's it, sit down."

She tried to focus on Coralee's face, but the lighting was wrong or something.

"Take a deep breath," David commanded.

She had been holding it in. Now it tore from her body in ragged gasps.

The voices swirled around her, words floating meaninglessly in the air, "Out – surface – some – can't handle – claustrophobic – no, don't think…"

She was walking, falling, someone carrying her. The engine revved up, the truck shifting into gear, driving uphill.

Jessie could feel her breathing slowing, but she was shivering uncontrollably, feeling cold from the inside out. Now she could feel Coralee's arm around her, hear her voice speaking gently, telling her it was going to be okay, to just hold on.

David's voice was laced with anxiety. "We're almost there. Just a little bit further."

At the surface now, light flooded in from the garage. They were helping her inside the house – back to the normalcy of the kitchen, the dining room, the fireplace.

Coralee wrapped a thick down comforter around her; David stacked more wood on the fire; and Martha brought her a steaming cup of hot chocolate.

The shivering gradually stopped, but in its place came a fatigue, draining her strength and weighing down her eyelids.

David had his stethoscope, listening to her heart and lungs. He took her temperature and asked her how she felt now.

"Just tired," Jessie mumbled.

"I'll help you take her up to bed, Coralee," Martha offered.

They helped her to stand, and David kissed Jessie on the cheek, looking worried. "You get yourself some rest, okay?"

Jessie slept late and woke up still feeling tired. Deciding what to wear seemed too complicated, so she put on the same clothes that she'd worn the day before.

She wasn't hungry and didn't want to be around anyone, but they'd already been to her door several times. She'd heard them whispering, obviously concerned that she was still asleep so late in the morning. Jessie sighed. She'd have to make an appearance sooner or later.

Standing at the top of the stairs watching the scene below, it seemed to Jessie as if everyone was busy getting ready for the wedding, laughing, talking, and scurrying about like ants at a picnic.

"I think I have some tape in my room," Martha called out and headed toward the stairs.

"Jessie, honey," she said in surprise, stopping as she caught sight of her.

Everyone else in the room stopped too, and stared up at her. Jessie resisted the urge to run back to her room. She had to face them sometime.

"G-good morning," she said in a shaky voice, starting down the stairs toward Martha.

David was across the room and up the stairs in an instant. "How are you feeling?" he asked in a quiet urgent voice.

"I'm fine." Jessie laughed nervously. "Sorry about last night."

"It's okay," David quickly reassured her. "It hits people that way sometimes, being underground." He looked closely at her. "As long as you're okay now."

"I'm fine." Jessie tried to sound confident and even managed a smile.

Martha had joined them. "Come into the kitchen, honey and I'll fix you a nice breakfast. I just pulled some cinnamon buns out of the oven."

Jessie pasted another smile on her face and walked down the rest of the stairs, concentrating on each step, not looking at the people around her.

Martha bustled around, pouring coffee and buttering a bun for Jessie. The coffee went down okay but the cinnamon bun stuck in her throat a little. Jessie ended up leaving most of it on her plate.

"Mr. Peters wanted me to ask you if you needed anything done."

Jessie looked up to see Colin standing in the doorway.

"No," Martha said, "I don't reckon there is anything right now, Colin." Then she paused and added, "It's such a lovely day; maybe you and Jessie would like to go for a walk. There aren't any other young people here her age."

Colin looked at Jessie, waiting for a response.

"You could take some of these cinnamon buns to your grandpa," Martha prompted.

Jessie sighed and stood to her feet. At least Colin didn't talk nonstop.

They walked through a passageway that led out outside to the end of a deck and a set of steps. Jessie realized that this was where she had run outside the morning before when the ladies had been talking about their babies.

"This sun should help the ice a lot."

Jessie paused halfway down the steps and looked at Colin beside her. "The sun will help the ice?"

He grinned and explained. "What I mean is that it will help the ice melt."

Jessie looked out over the still-frozen expanse. "You mean that it might melt today?"

"No," he said. "It won't go that fast."

There were halfway to Grandpa Pipe's cabin when a small boy rounded the corner and came into view. His hair was matted and his clothes ragged and dirty. She heard Colin speak his name almost as a sigh, "Joshua."

He looked to be about three or four, so Jessie was surprised to hear Colin ask him why he wasn't in school.

"I'm hungry," Joshua answered simply.

Colin knelt down beside him. "Where's Auntie?" he asked in a surprisingly gentle voice.

"Asleep," the little boy said, wiping his nose with the back of his hand.

Colin sighed and shook his head slightly. "C'mon, we'll have a little breakfast at Grandpa Pipe's house."

Joshua cheered up considerably and ran a little ahead of them as they continued on their way.

"He's your nephew?" Jessie asked quietly.

"No," Colin said in a flat voice, "my foster brother."

"But you asked him about your aunt. Won't your mother want to know he's not in –"

Colin stopped. His voice was hard. "She's not *my* aunt. My mother is dead. *I* was the foster child in his family but now his mother is dead and his father is in jail." He stopped speaking then, realizing that Joshua had turned back and was now within hearing distance.

Colin's pace increased in his agitation, and Jessie had to hurry to keep up. They turned off the main path and, as Pipe's house came into view, Joshua ran on ahead again.

"I'm sorry." She got close enough to Colin to speak in a low voice.

He shrugged it off and then they were at the door and Grandpa Pipe was greeting them with a big smile, ushering them into the cozy little cabin.

When Pipe got a little basin of warm water so Joshua could wash his hands, the little boy kept his hands immersed longer than necessary and Jessie realized they must have been cold. Colin found him a tissue to wipe his nose with, and Pipe said something to them that Jessie didn't understand. Colin moved over to one of the walls and took a small jacket from where it hung.

"Used to be mine," he told Jessie. Pipe seemed to be expressing his approval, speaking to Joshua and smiling as the little boy tried on the hooded, fleece jacket. It was a good fit and it was obvious that Joshua was very pleased with the gift.

The cinnamon bun he was given was quite large, but Joshua ate the whole thing, barely pausing for breath. Jessie and Pipe ate half of one apiece but Colin just sipped on his tea and watched Joshua eat.

The little boy's hands were washed again, and after speaking to Pipe, Colin wrapped another bun and put it in Joshua's pocket. "For recess," he said. "Now, get going to school so you can get really smart. Maybe become a doctor or lawyer or something."

Joshua flashed a grin at them as he ran for the door, called out "Bye-bye!" and was gone.

"He looks too young to be in school," Jessie ventured curiously.

"He's six years old," Colin answered shortly.

"But…" Jessie began.

"He doesn't get enough food sometimes." The tone of Colin's voice ended the subject.

Pipe was looking at them thoughtfully. Jessie watched as he tapped out his pipe and carefully refilled it. There was something calming about his actions. Or maybe it was just Pipe himself. Jessie didn't know if she'd ever met anyone before who seemed so much at peace.

He said something to Colin, and Colin interpreted for Jessie. "He wants to know if we saw any more birds with mustaches."

Pipe's eyes were twinkling and Jessie wondered if she would ever know for sure if they were stringing her a line or not. Was it really possible to tell a male pileated woodpecker from a female by its mustache?

Colin was shaking his head and Jessie assumed he was telling his grandpa that they hadn't seen any birds at all on the way today.

The pipe was lit and Colin poured fresh tea for everyone. Colin's grandpa had a relaxed, "story mode" sound to his voice as he spoke.

"The eagle is a smart bird too," Colin interpreted.

Jessie relaxed, took another sip of tea, and listened as Pipe talked about the way eagles made their nests and took care of their young.

But then a question was directed toward her.

"He's asking if you know how a female eagle chooses her mate."

Jessie shook her head. Why was he asking her?

Pipe topped off everyone's cup of tea before describing the intricate dance that the male and female performed during mating. "But all the time," Colin interpreted, "the female is deciding if this fellow is going to be a good father for her babies. He needs to be able to dive quickly and catch the baby eagles as they come out of the nest. All the time, she's thinking about if he will be a good father."

Jessie was feeling more uncomfortable by the minute. Pipe seemed to be directing all of his lecture toward her and with an intensity that would have been alarming if Pipe's voice was not also filled with compassion. But the old man couldn't know. He couldn't!

"Eagles only choose one mate for life," Colin continued to interpret, a puzzled look on his face. "The mother eagle makes sure that the father will take good care of their baby eagles."

"What if he's a jerk?" Jessie exploded, standing up and shouting the words. "What if he doesn't want to take care of his baby?"

"Jessie?" Colin was too alarmed by her words to interpret them to Pipe.

The old man was sitting there calmly smoking but there was a look of compassion in his eyes.

Jessie pushed away her chair, not caring that it fell with a clatter onto the linoleum floor. She yanked open the door of the cabin and fled into the crisp morning air.

Chapter Six

Jessie was half way up the path heading back to the main trail when Colin caught up with her. She swung around to confront him.

"What is he – some kind of witch doctor or something?"

Colin's jaw tightened. "We would say 'medicine man' and, no, Grandpa Pipe is about as far away as you can get from that. He's a Christian and has been for most of his life."

All the fight went of Jessie and she felt as if she were going to cry.

"There's a spot where I like to go sometimes," Colin said gently. "We can go there if you want."

Jessie nodded, swallowing back the tears and walking silently beside him as he led her toward a large flat rock down by the lake.

"I used to come here sometimes after my parents died," Colin said, looking out over the water.

Jessie's heart beat like a hammer. Could she tell someone after all?

"I – I'm expecting a baby," she blurted out, before she could lose her courage.

Colin blinked in surprise but when he turned to face her, his expression was more thoughtful than shocked.

"And the father," he echoed the words she had spoken in the cabin, "doesn't want to take care of his baby."

Jessie looked away.

"You've told him?" Colin asked quietly, though it was more of a statement.

Jessie gritted her teeth. "Of course I did." She hesitated. "I – I should have told him sooner, I guess. I kept thinking maybe I'd made a mistake or maybe something else was wrong with me. Then," Jessie bowed her head. "I was afraid to tell him."

Colin was silent for a moment. "So he told you he wouldn't help take care of the baby?"

"Yes!" Jessie spat out; then she added, "But he didn't have the guts to tell me straight out. He gave me some line about having to think about it – said he needed time."

Colin was looking out over the lake again. "Maybe he does needs time."

His words had been softly spoken, but Jessie felt them as a strong rebuke.

Her response was anger. "What do you know anyway? You're probably even younger than I am."

Colin stood to his feet. "I hope you are older than I am," he said in a quiet voice.

"What do you mean by that?" Jessie demanded. "You think I'm not old enough to be a good mother? Is that it? So how old are you anyway?"

"Fifteen," Colin said in the same calm, quiet voice.

Jessie sneered. "Just a kid – a know-it-all kid! Think you have all the answers to life. You don't know a thing."

Colin turned to go.

"Come to think of it, shouldn't you be in school, too?" Jessie demanded peevishly.

She barely heard his muttered reply. "Night school."

Jessie watched him walk away. Night school. He must have dropped out or been kicked out of high school and was taking evening classes somewhere.

Jessie knew she should go after him and apologize. But she felt rooted to the rock, weighed down by that heavy fatigue that she had felt the night before. The sky was gray and the lake beneath it reflected its gloom. Jessie stared out over the wide expanse and let her thoughts drift across its frozen barrens.

"There you are!"

Jessie groaned in frustration as Coralee approached. Was there no privacy in this place?

"Hey, girl, I've been looking all over for you."

Jessie attempted a smile and Coralee took this as an invitation to sit down beside her. "We were expecting you back for lunch and when you didn't come, we thought maybe you and Colin had eaten at his grandpa's house. But then Pipe brought some fish over to the lodge and said he hadn't seen either of you since before lunch."

Jessie remained silent, looking out at the lake again as Coralee droned on. "David was getting worried about you, but he and Dad were in the middle of building a trellis for the flowers so I said I'd go look for you."

So now you found me.

"David said you were really good with colors and such."

Jessie sighed and turned toward her.

"I thought maybe you could help us with the flowers," Coralee said hesitantly.

Jessie sighed again, nodded briefly, and stood to her feet.

Coralee, thankfully, was not as talkative on the way back. When they arrived at the lodge, everyone seemed content that Jessie had been found, and for the most part they demanded very little of her.

Martha did insist that she have something to eat and Jessie obligingly took a couple of bites from the sandwich that was set beside her. She sat in an easy chair by the fireplace, close enough to Coralee and her decorating efforts to be considered a part of it, but she was not, after all, consulted about the flowers.

She must have dozed off, because David's angry voice startled her awake. "Found him passed out under the deck!"

Jessie looked over to see who the object of this tirade was.

Colin! Jessie gave an involuntary cry at the sight of him. His clothes and hair were a mess as if he'd been lying in the mud, but it was his bowed head and the look of defeat in his eyes that made him look like a drunk.

"Just what do ya think you're doin'?" Tom's voice boomed out across the room, dwarfing David's. Jessie thought at first that the words were being directed to Colin, but Tom was glaring at David as he strode across the room. "Ya don't parade another man's faults in front of his friends!"

Then, as suddenly as it had appeared, the anger was gone and Tom's voice became remarkably gentle as he spoke to Colin. "C'mon son, we'll get you cleaned up and you can sleep it off." Tom's voice faded as he led Colin through the kitchen toward a guest bedroom and bathroom.

An uncomfortable silence descended on the room. David walked over to Jessie. "He wasn't drunk when he was with you, was he?"

Jessie shook her head and turned away.

David sat down in the sofa adjacent to her, a bundle of nervous energy. Coralee came and laid a gentle hand on his shoulder, and Jessie could see him visibly relax.

Jessie put her head on the arm of the chair and closed her eyes.

"I like the symbolism of eagles, don't you?"

Jessie jerked her head up. Someone else was sitting on the sofa where David had been – Coralee's brother, Jeff. And he wasn't talking to Jessie but to his mother. She was arranging some flowers around a white trellis archway. Jeff had a book open on his lap.

Martha turned to smile at him. "Yes," she said, "Isaiah 40:31 is one of my favorite verses."

Jeff lifted the book and read aloud: "They who wait upon the Lord will get new strength. They will rise up with wings like eagles. They will run and not get tired. They will walk and not become weak."

Jessie savored the words, wondering at their meaning. She had been feeling so tired lately. It would be good to have new strength, to soar like an eagle, to run and not be tired.

"And I really like the verse about Him carrying us on eagles' wings," Martha continued. "For those times when we're too weary to fly, he carries us."

"Hmm," Jeff mused, flipping pages. "Somewhere in Exodus isn't it. Oh, here it is, Exodus 19:4."

Jessie closed her eyes again and imagined how it would feel to be on an eagle's soft feathers, soaring high above the clouds, the sun warm on her back.

"Hey, sleepyhead," a teasing voice sounded close to Jessie's ear.

David.

"Every time I turn around, you're catching some more z's. Aren't you sleeping well, Jess? Strange bed, I guess, or maybe jet lag or something."

"I'm just a little tired, is all." Jessie yawned and tried to focus on her brother's face. But she was more than a little tired; she was a *lot* tired.

He put one hand on her forehead and another on her wrist. "Maybe you caught a flu bug on the trip." He knelt down to be at eye level with her. "I'm kinda concerned about you, kiddo."

"I'm just tired," Jessie mumbled.

"Well, I think I'll order some blood work for you tomorrow." David spoke decisively. He frowned at her. "You are eating properly aren't you?"

Jessie mumbled some non-committal answer.

"Well, it's supper time now. Maybe some of Martha's good home cooking will perk you up."

Jessie rose wearily to follow him as he continued, "A couple of the other ladies made some contributions too. I think Jenny made a pie."

His voice was lost in the larger cacophony of voices around the table. Jessie felt overwhelmed and eventually tuned them all out. She managed a few bites, picking listlessly at the food while supporting her head up with her other arm. Her eyes drifted shut.

"Jessie. Jessie."

She opened her eyes and looked blurrily at Coralee.

"I'm going to help you upstairs, Jess," Coralee said, guiding her away from the table toward the staircase. "Tomorrow, David's going to take you over to the clinic."

The clinic. Then everyone will know. Jessie bit her lip, feeling as though she might suddenly laugh hysterically – or cry.

Thankfully, Coralee didn't linger, staying just long enough to help Jessie take her shoes off and to lay a blanket over her and dim the lights.

The clinic – tomorrow – the clinic – tomorrow…

Jessie shuddered. What would her brother think of her when he found out the truth? What would the rest of them think? This fine group of people who prayed before meals and talked about verses in the Bible.

Jessie threw off the covers and sat up. Carrying her shoes, she tiptoed out of the room and down the hall to the bedroom with the secret staircase.

Outside, the moon was almost full, and the ice of the lake sparkled a little as she drew closer. Jessie looked out over the ice and trees and sky and felt as if she was all alone in a dark world of ice and snow. Tears began to fill her eyes.

"You're not wearing a jacket again," Colin's teasing voice sounded from behind her. "Here, take mine – again."

Jessie whirled around. "It's not funny!" she sobbed. "It's not funny!"

She turned and ran away from him towards the lake. Half way down the dock, she realized she needed to stop but suddenly there was a patch of ice beneath her feet and she was sliding and falling.

The fragile ice surface shattered like glass beneath her and in an instant she was immersed in a slushy ice and water mix that chilled deep into every bone and tissue.

Jessie felt disoriented in the darkness, unsure even of which way was up. She hated opening her eyes under water but forced herself to do it and finally saw a bit of light off to her right. She tried to swim toward it, but her sodden clothing was pulling her down.

She managed only a few strokes before her limbs felt too heavy to move.

Growing weaker already – and now her lungs were demanding air!

Something dragging me down!

Won't let me go!

I don't want to die! I don't want to die!

Let me go! Let me go!

AIR!

I'm coughing! I'm breathing!

David?

"Grab hold of her arms, Tom. I'll boost her up. Colin, you can let go now."

"Let go now, son. We've got her. It's okay."

"Grab him! He's going under!"

"She's breathing fine. Just put her on her side there."

"Help me with Colin."

The voices swirling around her made no sense to Jessie.

David's voice rose above the others. He was crying and saying her name over and over.

Maybe she was dead. But she couldn't be – not when she was going to be sick.

Someone turned her over as she threw up what felt like a gallon of water. "It's okay, Jess. You're okay now, hon," Coralee's voice – and someone putting a blanket around her.

"We're going to carry you up to the lodge now."

Jessie heard them helping Colin, too. He must have been the one to rescue her.

Jessie had the feeling that time had passed, but she couldn't be sure. The voices had faded – but they were back now. Had they ever stopped?

"So tell me again exactly what happened."

"David, he needs to rest."

"Keep out of it, Jeff. She's my sister!"

Jessie heard a sigh, then a voice so weak, she didn't at first recognize it as Colin's. "She ran off the end of the dock – and I went in after her."

"And just why would my sister jump off the dock onto ice barely thick enough to support a – a mouse?" David demanded.

"I think maybe she wanted to die," Colin said in that same barely audible voice. "She asked me a lot of questions about the ice and how thick it was and how easy it would be for someone to fall through – and drown."

"No!"

David's vehement denial was met with only silence.

"Jessie wouldn't do that!" He protested again.

"She's going to have a baby," came the weary reply.

"What did you say?" David shouted. "What did you say?"

"He said she's pregnant." Jeff's voice was gentle, and so was his touch as he lifted Jessie's wrist and spoke her name.

"We're going to move you over to the health center, Jessie. Can you hear me? Just squeeze my hand a little if you can hear."

Yes, she could do that. But she was too tired to talk to David. Too tired.

"Don't fight it. Just let yourself wake up slow. You're at the health center." The woman's soothing voice continued, "You won't be alone. I'll be right here beside you."

Jessie felt herself relaxing a little as the voice continued. She began to realize it was Martha speaking to her. "Your mother is on her way. She was coming anyway for the wedding, but she's going to try to make some better connections and get here by this evening."

She's going to be so mad! She'll never ever forgive me.

"Don't worry," Martha reassured her. "David only told her that you had fallen through the ice; he didn't tell her about your pregnancy."

That was something anyway. Still she'd find out soon enough.

"Don't be too hard on your brother, hon," Martha continued. "He's been so keyed up about the wedding, and he was so excited about you coming up here. I think maybe things could have been – should have been – different. We – none of us – have been as supportive as we could have been. But the wedding's been postponed now –"

"No!" She wanted to shout the word but it had come out as a hoarse whisper.

Martha's gentle smile was reassuring and her voice kind. "Take a little sip of water, honey."

It did feel good to have a drink, but the simple effort of drawing water up through the straw left her exhausted. Jessie closed her eyes again.

"That's right. You just rest now."

Jessie could feel the blankets being tucked up around her.

"Oh, I almost forgot," Martha said cheerily. "One of your friends from back home called. He sounded quite concerned that you weren't up to talking to him." Martha patted her hand. "As soon as you're feeling a bit better, we'll move a phone into your room so that you can receive calls. But for now, it's important that you get all the rest you can. We want to take care of that little baby of yours."

The baby.

She felt a flicker of movement then, but the twinge of pain was no match for the twisting, tearing force that thrust its way up pushing against her throat, making it impossible to cry out – impossible to breathe.

"Just let it go child. Let it go."

The wail burst out of her with a violence that tore at her lungs and burned her throat.

"It's okay to cry, honey. Just let it all out."

Martha gently pushed back the strands of wet hair clinging to her face, and continued to speak soft soothing words. Jessie's sobs subsided but the tears continued to fall.

"She's been like this for over an hour, Jeff. Isn't there something we can do?" Martha's voice hovered somewhere close by.

"I don't want to risk using a sedative. We're not sure that she's fully conscious yet – and the baby…"

The baby.

"Her body's gone through a severe trauma and with the added complication of a pregnancy…" Jeff left the sentence hanging then added more briskly, "Just keep talking to her. It does seem to have a calming effect."

"Jessie, honey, it's Martha. Did I tell you that your mother will be here soon? We got a call that she should be in on the evening flight. She's in Winnipeg. Do you remember when you were there – just a few days ago?"

Just a few days ago! It felt like an eternity.

"She's focusing a little! Jessie."

Jeff's face swam into view and she heard his words: "How're you feeling, Jessie?"

She tried to answer but her mouth felt as dry as cotton.

Martha held a straw to her lips and Jessie drank deeply of the cool water.

They were staring expectantly at her, and Jessie felt she should attempt a smile. Her weak effort was rewarded with huge enthusiastic grins from both Jeff and his mother. "Looks like our patient is recovering," Jeff said cheerily, glancing at the flashing monitors beside her bed and then back to Jessie again. "I think there's an anxious brother that I should go have a little word with."

David!

Jeff was already gone before she could speak the word aloud.

But Martha heard. "I sent him back to his cabin to rest, honey. It was tearin' him up watchin' you and waiting." The older woman paused. "He'll be glad to see you're doing better now."

Jessie nodded and tried another smile.

"But your eyes are still waterin' child," Martha said gently. "I've changed your pillow twice already in the last hour."

"I – I can't…"

"It's all right, child. It's all right."

Jessie closed her eyes, letting the tears fall unheeded.

"Maybe…" Martha stroked back the wet strands of hair. "Maybe if you talked about it."

Jessie resisted the urge to pick at the bandage covering the IV needle on the back of her hand. She couldn't tell them. She just couldn't.

"You'd hate me," she whispered. "All of you – especially David."

"Jessie." Martha leaned toward her. "I don't think there's anything you could ever do that would make David stop loving you. He's been so worried about you these past few days. And he didn't think twice about jumping into that icy water; neither did Colin." Martha reached out to hold Jessie's trembling hands. "You have a lot of people here who care very much what happens to you. A lot of prayers have been going up on your behalf."

Jessie shook her head and turned away.

"Honey-child." The endearment was spoken with a tenderness that Jessie couldn't ignore. Her eyes met Martha's and were held by them. "Love is a gift that must be received. You have to open up your heart and let that love in, Jessie."

"No." The word was like a sob that caught in Jessie's throat, making further speech impossible.

Martha's hand on hers was warm. "Someone you trusted hurt you."

It was spoken as a statement, but Jessie had not the strength nor desire to deny it. Martha continued gently. "People will let us down. But don't close your heart, child. There are others who love you very, very much."

Jessie looked up into the kind eyes and for a moment, could almost believe that her words were true.

"David and Colin risked their lives to jump in after you," Martha continued. "But Jessie, there's someone else who knew ahead of time that He would die but He loved you so much that He freely gave His life so that you could be saved."

"Somebody died?" Jessie cried out.

Not David – or Colin. Maybe Tom then or…?

"Jesus, honey," Martha said quickly. "It was Jesus who died so that you might live – forever."

Jessie blinked. "I – I knew that."

Martha smiled gently. "You know what He did, but do you know Him?"

Jessie hesitated. "I – I don't think so."

"He's a good friend – the best you'll ever have."

Jessie closed her eyes and pulled her hand away, blocking out Martha's tender smile and warm touch.

"Jessie." Martha persisted.

At that moment, something exploded deep within her, and Jessie shouted hoarsely, "I'm gonna get an abortion! How's that going to go over with all you kind, loving people? What's David going to think of me then?"

Chapter Seven

The love and compassion in Martha's eyes didn't change. If anything, it seemed to intensify! And suddenly it was enough.

Love – unconditional, unmerited love – was being offered to her, and Jessie reached for it as for a drink of water in a desert.

She had been thirsty for so long!

Then, just as suddenly, the fears came rushing back. "There's no way out. There's nothing I can do. I don't want this baby and I don't want to have a child that isn't loved – isn't wanted."

Martha was still listening, nodding her understanding, and Jessie stumbled on, "My – my mother never wanted any more children. She had David when she was just seventeen and she told me once that was the only reason she married our dad. She didn't like kids. They interfered with her career. She took the pill for years – but she must have got careless – or forgot, or something – and then…"

"And then you were born," Martha finished in a tender voice.

Jessie nodded, once more too overcome for speech.

Tears glistened in Martha's eyes as she opened the drawer of the bedside table, took out a Gideon Bible and began to flip through the pages. "A long while ago – actually a few thousand years ago – there was a young man named David. His father and his brothers didn't have a very high opinion of him. He was the youngest in this family and he got the jobs nobody else wanted to do. But," Martha paused for emphasis, "David came to understand that to God, he was not an extra burden or a mistake. It's actually part of a song that he wrote. It's found in Psalm 139, verses thirteen to sixteen." Martha lifted the Bible and began to read:

> For You made the parts inside me. You put me together inside my mother.
>
> I will give thanks to You, for the greatness of the way I was made brings fear. Your works are great and my soul knows it very well.
>
> My bones were not hidden from You when I was made in secret and put together with care in the deep part of the earth.
>
> Your eyes saw me before I was put together. And all the days of my life were written in Your book before any of them came to be.

"Jessie," Martha continued, "God made you. He was the one who put you together, who lovingly fashioned each part of you. He arranged all the genes so that you would have beautiful dark hair and brown eyes and a sweet smile –"

"And a fiery hot temper," David's voice sounded from the doorway. "No one can stomp their foot quite like my little sister."

"David!" Jessie felt a surge of joy.

"Hey, little sis. Back in the land of the living, I see."

"I'll leave you two to visit," Martha said and quietly slipped out of the room.

In the ensuing silence, both David and Jessie were suddenly at a loss for words. Jessie looked at him, sitting hunched over in the chair beside her bed. His eyes were red and swollen, and his usually immaculate clothes were wrinkled and worn as if he'd slept the night in them – or not slept.

And his hands were bandaged.

"David." She spoke hesitantly, her eyes fixed on the white strips of gauze.

He seemed a little embarrassed as he followed her gaze to his hands. "I sorta panicked, I guess. I imagined you just under the surface of the ice trying to break through. It – it was such a horrible thought. I broke a lot of ice before realizing that it wasn't helping us to find you. Then Colin appeared." David's voice grew even quieter. "He was holding onto you with one arm and trying to push his way through the ice with his other. He – he looked as if he was at the end of his strength. I owe him a lot." David's voice trailed off into a whisper and his head remained bowed.

Jessie thought about the debt she owed Colin. He had risked his own life to save hers. But David had risked his as well, and without his help, both Colin and she would likely have drowned.

And in that moment, Jessie knew that it was not David who had failed her. It was her expectations that had been wrong. He would have given his life for her – he almost did – but he would never help her get an abortion.

She'd always counted on him to fix whatever was wrong. But Jessie knew that this time, he wouldn't – couldn't – fix what was wrong. Jessie turned her head away. No one could fix it.

"I was so afraid that you were – were not going to make it." David's voice broke and Jessie turned quickly back toward him. Her brother crying?

"David." She spoke his name in a whisper, realizing for the first time the awful pain he was feeling on her behalf. She hadn't thought about what effect her death would have had on him.

David's voice was husky as he stumbled on. "I'm sorry that I wasn't there for you, Jess. I was thinking about the wedding. I was worried about you, but I just didn't take the time to – to find out what was wrong." He bowed his head again. "I should have listened. I should have taken the time to listen to you."

"No, David," Jessie said emphatically. "It wasn't your fault. There was nothing you could have done. There's nothing you can do." Jessie's voice trailed off.

The warmth in his voice drew her eyes up to his. "I'm not going to let you quit, Jess. We're going to get through this thing together. I'm going to be there for you all the way, whatever it takes. We've postponed the wedding –"

"You shouldn't have!" Jessie exclaimed. "Coralee was so excited. The flowers and the cake –"

"The flowers and the cake can be replaced," David said firmly. "You," his voice softened, "you are irreplaceable."

"Coralee…"

David shook his head. "She's the one that suggested it in the first place. I – I was incapable of making any decisions at all. If – if you had died…" Fresh tears began to fall as he asked hesitantly, "Colin said you – you did it on purpose?"

"No!" Jessie exclaimed. "I was running on the dock and I slipped on some ice."

"Really?" David was eager to believe it.

"Yes," Jessie assured him. "I'm not saying that the thought didn't cross my mind, but I never got as far as making a plan or anything."

David looked so relieved that Jessie felt overwhelmed with guilt that she had put her brother through so much worry. "I'm sorry," she said.

David reached over and hugged her. "It's okay, Jess. As long as you're okay now."

"I'm okay now," Jessie said, at least half meaning it.

David sat back in his chair. "I really missed you. Four years is a long time."

"I missed you, too."

It had been especially difficult the first couple of years. She and her mother had moved more times than Jessie could count, and it had been hard to make friends – harder still to keep them. She'd learned how to buy "friends" with gifts and favors. Her mother had given her free rein with a credit card and had certainly had no concern at all about how she spent her time!

But what she'd really missed was having someone to love her. Then she'd met Robert.

"Who did this to you, Jess?" David's concern for her put an edge to his voice.

But Jessie shook her head. "No one did it *to me*, David. We were both responsible, Robert and I."

"Robert." David almost spat the word.

"It was my fault really. I didn't like the side effects of being on the pill so I stopped taking it."

"He should have waited." David's voice softened. "You both should have waited, Jess."

"I – I thought it would help me to keep him. I didn't want to lose him." The ache in Jessie's throat made further words impossible.

"And you have lost him," David said with more sadness than condemnation in his voice.

"Colin says that I should give him more time."

"Colin?" David frowned. "How much time have you given him, Jess?"

"It was…" Jessie began hesitantly. "I told him maybe three or four days before I came up here."

David shook his head. "There's something I don't understand. You don't look very pregnant – at least, you hid it pretty well with bulky sweaters. But, Jessie, you were still – with this fellow – up until a few days before you left and," David lifted his eyebrows expressively, "he didn't notice that you were expecting a baby?"

Jessie smiled wryly. "A few months ago, Robert had this conversion experience – said he gave his heart to Jesus or something like that. And he did this big thing about telling me he was sorry and asking my forgiveness and saying he wanted to stay pure from now on." Jessie lowered her eyes. "He said that he loved me still but –"

"Wait a minute!" David interrupted. "This guy's a Christian? The father of your baby is a Christian? And he expected you to have an abortion, I suppose? How he could call himself a Christian –"

Jessie shook her head and turned away. "The abortion is my idea," she whispered.

Jessie felt him pull away from her physically and knew that he was withdrawing emotionally too. Well, she had known what his reaction would be – had known ever since she'd realized what he'd been up to these past few years. He would never even recommend another doctor for her. And she'd waited too long now. It would be almost impossible for her to find someone to do the job this late in the pregnancy.

"Why did you wait so long?" David's voice sounded distant.

Why *had* she waited so long?

Jessie turned over, bending her legs and wrapping her arms around her chest. She felt cold and miserable, and her stomach hurt. It hurt a lot.

The footsteps echoing across the floor weren't a surprise. She'd driven him away; she knew that. And she had no more tears to spend – no more strength left even to cry.

But the door swung open again and the same familiar quick steps were heard, this time approaching her bed. Jessie felt a blanket being lowered over top of her – and then another.

"Better?"

Jessie looked up into David's eyes. There was a sadness and a resignation in them, but, without any shadow of doubt, there was also love.

"You seemed cold."

Jessie smiled weakly. "Thanks."

David sat down again.

"Jessie," he began hesitantly, "ever since you came up here, I've been wanting to tell you something. I'm – I'm not very good at this. I haven't had much opportunity to tell anyone who didn't already know. We're kind of isolated up here."

Jessie was growing alarmed. "David."

He laughed nervously. "It's nothing bad. It's actually something very wonderful. You see, I met Someone –"

"Besides Coralee?"

"No, no, I don't mean like another woman." David sighed. "Jessie, we've never been religious in our family. I mean, I did take you to catechism class. Mom and Dad both agreed on that, at least. But that's as far as it went. Then when I came here, I started to learn more about who Jesus really is and –"

"Not you, too!"

David lifted an eyebrow and grinned. "'Fraid so."

"I thought you were just fitting in – you know, bowing your head to pray when they did and stuff."

David smiled sardonically. "As in, 'When in Rome…'" He shook his head. "It was like that at first. But I guess I started to realize that this God they were serving might just be real." David's voice rose enthusiastically. "And if He was…!"

77

"Yes?" Jessie asked faintly.

David leaned forward, his eyes shining with excitement. "Jessie, don't you see? I can know the One who made me. I can know why He made me. I can be in partnership with Him. My life can have meaning and purpose!"

"What can I say?" Jessie responded without enthusiasm. "I'm really happy for you."

"Jessie, He wants to be your friend."

"How do you know what God wants or doesn't want?"

David picked up the Bible that Martha had set down. "It's right in here, Jess. I'll read it for you if you like."

Jessie shrugged. David took this as an affirmative response and began to flip through the pages until he found the spot. "It's in the first book of John in the fourth chapter, verses, nine to thirteen. Here's what it says:

God has shown His love to us by sending His only Son into the world. God did this so we might have life through Christ. This is love! It is not that we loved God but that He loved us. For God sent His Son to pay for our sins with His own blood.

Dear friends, if God loved us that much, then we should love each other. No person has ever seen God at any time. If we love each other, God lives in us. His love is made perfect in us. He has given us His Spirit. This is how we live by His help and He lives in us.

Jessie shook her head. "It's different for you, David. You spent four years of your life rescuing babies." Jessie lowered her voice. "I want to kill mine."

He winced slightly but shook it off. "I did spend four years of my life here with Rachel's Children, and through our efforts, hundreds of babies that would have died are instead living. And it grieves me more than I can tell you to think that you would want to end your child's life. But Jessie, God doesn't love you any less or me any more because of what we've done or not done. The Bible says that God is love. It's as simple as that. He loves us no matter who we are or what we've done."

Jessie bowed her head.

"I was so scared."

"Jess?"

"In the water."

David nodded slowly. "I was scared for you."

"Would I – would I have gone to hell, David?"

David was silent a minute before answering in a quiet voice. "I don't know, Jess."

"I'm – I'm still afraid." And her stomach was hurting again.

"Jessie, you can talk to God. His arms are open, ready and waiting for you. He loves you."

"I'm afraid."

"Afraid of what, Jess? Tell me what you're afraid of."

"That – that..." Jessie paused, plumbing the depths of her soul, then spoke the words in a whisper, almost afraid to hear them herself. "That He won't be there – that He'll let me down." Jessie looked into David's eyes, saw understanding there and faltered on. "Colin's grandpa was telling us about eagles. The baby eagles are pushed out of the nest. That's how they learn to fly. But if they don't make it the first time, the daddy eagle is there to catch them."

"Jessie." He leaned toward her, speaking in a voice that was at once gentle but firm. "God is not like our dad."

"I know that," she said quickly, then stopped. How much *did* her past relationships effect how she viewed future ones?

"The Bible actually says that God will be a Father to the fatherless," David said. "And in another place, it says that

His name is Faithful and True. You can trust God with your life – and with your love."

"But what if He's not who you say He is – or maybe God's not even there. Maybe we just happened. Maybe everything's by chance – the luck of the draw."

David raised an eyebrow and grinned.

"Well, how do you know?" Jessie insisted.

"Quite simply," David shrugged, "you don't. It's a question of faith."

"Faith?"

"Mm, I'll read you another verse, here in Hebrews, chapter eleven, the first verse. It says, 'Now faith is being sure we will get what we hope for. It is being sure of what we cannot see.'"

"But how can you be sure of what you can't see?"

David grinned. "It takes faith."

Jessie rolled her eyes and sighed theatrically.

"Seriously though, Jess, it's a decision that you have to make – a decision to trust."

A decision to trust.

"Just talk to God," David invited. "Give Him a chance to prove Himself faithful."

Jessie hesitated only a moment longer until David said, "Pray with me." Then she bowed her head and closed her eyes.

David spoke first. "Dear precious Lord, this is my sister, Jess. She – she's been hurt a lot. People have let her down – and she's afraid to trust again. She's afraid to trust You. Please reveal Yourself to her, dear Lord. Surround her with Your love. Hold her in Your everlasting arms. Lift her up on eagles' wings."

Something stirred deep within her heart and Jessie felt a yearning to know this One who loved her so completely. When David invited her to pray, she was ready.

"God, I don't know much about You. David says I can trust You. He's pretty smart, but I guess this is one thing I've got to decide for myself. I do want to trust You. I need Your strength. I can't do this on my own. I – ohh!" Jessie broke off as a sharp pain gripped her.

David was instantly alert. "What is it? What's wrong?"

"My stomach – it's worse."

"Your stomach! Jessie, show me exactly where it hurts."

She put a hand on her swollen abdomen and found it rock hard. No, it couldn't be!

Chapter Eight

David understood the implications even better than Jessie did. With his hand still resting on her, he began to pray again, "Oh, Lord, we need your help now. Please protect this little life – and my sister."

When he opened his eyes, Jessie could see the deep concern in them. And she could hear it in his voice as he said, "I want you on complete bed rest. If you need anything, you ring this bell. We're already monitoring your baby's heartbeat – and yours. Jeff and I are the only doctors in the community right now. Our area of expertise is neonatal, so your baby's in good hands, but I'd feel a lot better if there was an obstetrician nearby."

"David."

He had been talking faster and faster and pacing as he spoke. When she said his name, it was as if someone had pulled the plug on his energy source. He walked toward her slowly and said in a halting voice, "You're in premature labor, Jess."

And it was strangely, at that moment, as David, once more galvanized into action, was hurrying from the room, that Jessie realized for the first time that she was carrying a live child. Gently she placed both hands on her now softer belly and spoke to the baby she had been carrying for six months.

"I'm sorry that I didn't want you. I do want you now. Please stay in there until you've grown a bit more. It's too early."

David burst through the door with an older Native woman behind him. Every hair in place, her professional-looking white blouse and black pants neatly pressed, she exuded confidence. Her expression, in complete contrast to David's, was one of total composure, and Jessie felt immediately reassured by her presence.

"This is Lillian," David said in a rush. "She's delivered more babies than most doctors. By the time a doctor flies in here or before a mother has a chance to fly out, often the baby is already born –"

"David," Lillian interrupted gently, "maybe you could just wait outside for a bit."

"What? Oh sure. I'll, umm, just wait outside."

The two women exchanged smiles as David headed for the door.

It was like the calm after a storm. Lillian moved competently, checking the IV, the fetal heart monitor, and Jessie's pulse and blood pressure. "When did the contractions start?" she asked in a soft but clear voice.

Jessie shook her head. "I'm not sure. I didn't really notice it at first. I thought maybe I had a stomachache or something."

Lillian patted her hand. "It's okay. Just tell me when you feel the next one."

But even as Jessie nodded her agreement, she could feel the pain building. "Now." She groaned. "Right now."

Lillian laid one hand gently on Jessie's abdomen and another on her shoulder. "Just breathe slow and easy." Her voice swept up and back down as Jessie breathed in and back out.

"And again," Lillian instructed.

Jessie looked gratefully at her mentor. With this woman by her side, it wouldn't be so difficult. But the next contraction came sooner and harder than either of them expected, and the next one wasn't far behind.

David returned between contractions and Jessie had her eyes closed. "How's it going?" she heard him ask.

The pain was building again. There'd hardly been time for her to catch her breath!

"Too quick." Lillian's voice was edged with concern. "The contractions are coming too quick."

"Jeff's on his way. I'll tell him to hurry. Jamie – we'll need Jamie."

David's voice faded.

The pain intensified.

It was as relentless as a battering ram, breaking her down, leaving her without the strength to mount a defense for the next assault.

Voices and faces appeared and disappeared as Jessie crested the waves of pain that threatened at any moment to drown her. She reached out for them, crying for help, begging them to do something – anything! She couldn't stand it any longer! She couldn't go through another contraction. She couldn't!

"Don't push yet," Lillian ordered.

But there was nothing that Jessie could do to stop it. Lillian's stern face swam into view, then was shut out as Jessie's body contorted, her muscles taut, crying out for release.

Space and time lost their meaning. Only pain remained, constant and relentless.

When they finally did urge her to push, she was too weak. Her body contracted but Jessie was nearing unconsciousness and could do nothing to progress the labor.

She had an awareness that something was required of her but she couldn't respond.

"Her vitals – we're losing her."

The words had surfaced out of the mist, clear for a moment, then receding again.

Jessie felt peace flowing over her, then a sensation of floating, being lifted up. Yes, carried on eagles' wings! The sun warm on her back, soft feathers beneath her. Light and love and joy – soaring joy!

"Stop! You can't do this!"

David's voice? No. Robert's! But it couldn't be!

"Get him out of here!"

David, this time for sure.

"If that baby dies, you'll answer to me!"

"Yeah and who are you?"

"I'm the father."

Jessie heard a loud crash and in the same instant felt the pain rise like a scream, drawing her body as tight as a bow, forcing the breath from her lungs in a long groan.

"Get him out of here!" David gasped.

"No!" Lillian's voice sounded close. "Her vitals are up. He stays."

Jeff was moving across the room as he said, "We *are* trying to save the baby's life. We might even be trying too hard."

Robert was struggling to catch his breath. "What – what do you mean?" His voice filled suddenly with fear. "Jessie!"

Jeff said in a calm and clear voice, "Her situation was precarious even before she went into premature labor. Her temperature and blood pressure haven't stabilized enough for us to risk putting her under for a C-section. I don't know if you're aware that Jessie was suffering from hypothermia."

Robert sounded near panic. "Hypothermia – cold – why?"

"Because of you!" David yelled from across the room.

Jeff's voice was still calm and even compassionate. "We need all the help we can get, David. Better cut him some slack."

Robert was speaking her name again in a trembling voice, but any response Jessie might have attempted was lost as another contraction tore through her body.

Lillian's voice was soft and low. "Try to push again."

"One good strong push; we'll have that baby out," Jeff encouraged.

David joined the others in cheering her on: "C'mon Jess! You can do it."

But when Robert spoke, all the other voices blurred and faded, and his alone rose sharply into focus. "For our baby, Jess! For our baby. Push hard! Push hard. For our baby! For our little baby.

"That's okay, Jess. Don't cry. The nurse says to rest. You need to build up your strength for the next contraction. Just rest now. Rest now."

She could feel him pushing the wet strands of hair off her forehead. His anxiety was causing him to speak fast, but he was keeping his voice low, and the sound of it was comforting to Jessie. "I've got a place for us. It's a basement apartment, but there's big windows and it's in a real nice section of town, and the lady that owns it is real nice – like somebody's grandma. It's mostly already furnished – some real nice old pieces of furniture. They're like antiques –

"I know it's building again. I can feel your stomach getting tight. Hold onto my hand, Jess. Squeeze as hard as you like. It's okay. Now you need to push. The doctor says he can see the top of the baby's head. Get ready, Jess. Okay, push! Push!"

Jessie heard a cheer go up in the room then Robert's voice close to her ear again. "Just one more push for the shoulders, Jess. You can do it."

There was a collective gasp as the baby was born; then silence.

Jessie felt an instant of profound relief, then in the next breath an anguish deeper than she could ever have imagined.

The baby's not crying! The baby's not crying!

Jessie forced up the leaden weights that were her eyelids, seeking for reassurance but finding an even greater fear flood over her as Robert's face swam into focus. She had never seen him so pale, so scared and defenseless.

He was averting his eyes. Was their baby dead?

Jessie struggled to speak but could barely manage a low whisper. "Robert."

As he turned his ravaged face slowly toward hers, Jessie regretted calling him. But she couldn't turn away.

"They're working on…" His voice broke and he turned with a hoarse cry. "Him or her? Is it him or her?"

Jessie felt a gentle touch on her shoulder and heard the calm reassurance in Lillian's voice. "You have a baby girl."

"Have?" Robert pleaded in a tearful voice.

Lillian rested her other hand on his shoulder. "The little lungs collapsed with her first breath. Babies that are born premature sometimes don't have a chemical called surfactant. They have what's called hyaline membrane disease. They're working on getting your little girl on a respirator –"

"She was all blue," Robert interrupted, "and she didn't cry."

Even as her fears intensified, Jessie felt a swell of gratitude toward him. Robert was expressing so exactly what she was feeling.

Lillian had been glancing occasionally off to her left. Suddenly Jessie saw the expression on her face change. The older nurse released her breath in a long sigh and tears began to roll down her weathered cheeks. Jessie closed her eyes, feeling the full weight of grief crush down upon her.

Lillian said something, but it didn't register on Jessie. Robert's heart-rending sobs filled her consciousness, so much in tune with Jessie's pain that it was indistinguishable from her own.

Jessie felt Lillian's hands resting gently on her cheeks, cupped under her chin, slowly drawing her attention toward the sound of her voice. The words, quietly insistent, broke through the barrier of grief Jessie had built up around her. "She's breathing. Your little girl is breathing."

Robert's sobs. Not grief then, but a breaking of the dam of emotions too long held back. In less than a week, he'd been told he was a father, had flown over a thousand miles not knowing what he might find at the end, and supported Jessie through a labor that had culminated in a life-and-death battle for their child. Jessie's own pain was lost as she reached out to comfort him. He looked up at her, and Jessie spoke his name, a tremulous smile on her lips.

Robert's chest still heaved and his voice was husky. "A baby girl."

"Yes." Jessie spoke the word in a sigh.

Robert clasped her hands tightly in his. Jessie felt the warmth of his love flowing through her. She closed her eyes, a smile still lingering on her lips.

She awoke to a silence so deep and profound as to be frightening. In the gray stillness, Jessie felt first pain and then loneliness.

Then she remembered.

"Jesus, my new friend," she prayed, "I am alone and afraid."

But then she wasn't any longer.

A deep peace enveloped her. Jessie closed her eyes again and forgot her pain as her thoughts rested upon her new baby daughter. What would they name her? *They.* It was more than she could have ever imagined – Robert here and so passionately caring for both her and their child.

"You're awake!"

The joy in his eyes touched something deep within her, and as he bent to kiss her, Jessie felt as though her heart might burst with love.

"Your child is still fighting for her life."

The words, sharply spoken, drove a wedge between them, piercing their sweet joy and robbing them of the comfort of companionship. Shame replaced the love that had so recently knit their hearts as one.

Jessie felt her throat constrict and could barely gasp his name. "David."

He had been about to leave but turned back at the sound of her voice.

"David, please..."

Jessie saw the deep lines of weariness in his face. His eyes had dark circles beneath them, and in the dimly lit room they were almost lost in shadow. He sank onto a stool by the foot of her bed, his shoulders sagging, his whole body drooping with weariness.

"Can – can I see her?" Robert spoke in a tentative voice.

David's eyes hardened. Then his face grew rigid, and Jessie watched in growing alarm as his fists clenched. Something was coming together in the back of her mind. The bruise on Robert's cheek. She must have at least subconsciously noted it before. And now she could see that blood had seeped through the bandages on David's right hand. He'd already struck Robert once!

"David!" She called in a hoarse whisper.

But all his attention was focused on Robert. David's voice was as hard and cold as ice. "You can look through the glass window of the nursery before you leave. There's a hotel if you want to sleep what's left of the night. Plane leaves at nine a.m." David stood up and motioned toward the door. "Now get out of my sister's room and get out of my sister's life."

"No!" Jessie gasped. But he was already walking away from her. David was gone. Robert was leaving!

"No!" she tried again, but her throat constricted and no sound came out. He was gone. Robert was gone!

She had to go after him! Had to somehow stop him and bring him back. David wouldn't stay angry for long. He couldn't – no, he couldn't – have meant what he said.

"Robert." Jessie's voice was a weak whisper and her legs trembled as she tried to stand – tried to go after him. She clung to the bed, then made an attempt to reach the door. But her weakened body betrayed her and she collapsed on the cold, tile floor. "David." The word rose like a sob as Jessie struggled forward a mere inch or two more before losing consciousness.

Shoes. Why was she looking at shoes? And a voice from far away – coming closer now. Someone calling her name.

A buzz of voices around her now. Meaningless noise. Robert's voice not among them.

Jessie felt herself being lifted and then lowered and then the warmth of blankets being wrapped around her and David's voice.

"Jess, I don't know if you can hear me. I – I'm sorry. I blew it again. It's just – it's just that I hate to see you go through all this. And it's too easy for me to put all the blame on your friend – Robert." David's voice rose, his words punctuated with emotion. "Jessie, I'll find him for you. We'll talk. All of us will talk."

"She needs to rest." A woman's voice came from the other side of the bed. "So do you, David."

There was a brief pause before he answered in a quiet but firm voice. "I'll find Robert first. Then I'll rest."

Then I'll rest too. Jessie didn't have the strength to even open her eyes, let alone speak but she willed David to find Robert – to bring him back.

Chapter Nine

It might have been minutes. It might have been hours. Jessie knew that time had passed and that she was awakening from sleep.

She heard them whispering anxiously and thought at first that her baby's condition might have worsened.

Then she heard Robert's name and recognized the apprehension in David's voice. "I already looked there, Jamie – and I've checked the hotel several times. The airport was locked up for the night, but I'll call there as soon as it opens."

"Where could he have gone?" Jamie wondered aloud.

David's voice was grim. "I don't know."

"Called the police yet?" A new voice that Jessie recognized as the nurse, Lillian, entered the conversation.

"Yes." David spoke the word in a barely audible voice, but it crashed like thunder on Jessie, making her heart race.

Why would they call the police? Did they think Robert was in some kind of trouble? How long had they been searching? How long had he been missing?

"It's been three hours." David unknowingly answered Jessie's question. "They're not too worried yet. It's not the middle of the winter and…" David's voice faltered. "I searched the shoreline. There's – there's no fresh holes – in the ice."

"You really thought...?" Jamie's voice was full of compassion.

"I don't know what I thought." David spoke heavily. "I would never have believed that Jessie could..." His voice dropped to a whisper again. "It still seems like some kind of nightmare."

"The radio station will be on soon," Lillian said.

Who cares if the radio's on or not! Jessie thought angrily.

"People would notice a stranger."

What is she talking about?

"That's a good idea," Jamie spoke up. "We should include a description – like hair color and what he was wearing."

"Red hair." David mused.

"And wasn't he wearing a black shirt?" Jamie asked. "And gray pants."

"But the black shirt was open," David interjected. "There was a T-shirt underneath. I think it might have been dark green."

"His hair is curly – cut fairly short." Jamie hesitated. "The bruise on his left cheek – it will still be there." She hurried on. "And I think his eyes are brown."

No, they're green.

Jessie found her voice. "Green," she said aloud.

They hurried to her side, two nurses and a doctor, anxious to assess her physical well-being. But the doctor was also her brother, and his thoughts went beyond the medical. Once again there had been a rift in their relationship, and David was full of remorse.

"It's okay," Jessie reassured him. "But Robert – why do you need his description? Why were you talking to the police about him?"

David rubbed his forehead. Jessie thought he looked more tired than ever. There was an easy chair beside her bed now. David slouched into it and Jessie could see that her energetic, and generally unflappable, brother was close to collapse. *He needs to sleep.*

"I looked everywhere," David said wearily. "Everywhere."

"Robert is probably somewhere safe and dry." Jamie glanced out the window as streaks of rain dashed against the pane. Her voice was clear and competent. "David is worried about him because he doesn't seem to be anywhere obvious, like the hotel or the lodge."

She was trying to be reassuring, but there was no getting away from the fact that Robert had gone missing in an isolated community in Northern Canada. At this time of year, the only way in or out was by air. To walk or drive out was impossible. Only in the winter were the surrounding muskeg and water frozen enough to travel on. In the summer, there were long portages. And he wouldn't know the way, in any case.

"He couldn't have gone far." Jessie struggled to keep her voice steady.

"People will be watching out for him now." Lillian's voice sounded from the door. "They'll put it on the community radio." She came closer and smiled at Jessie with kindness in her eyes. "People are talking of a search party. Right now it is just the police looking and," her voice softened, "many of us are also praying."

Jessie closed her eyes, feeling them begin to fill with tears. Yes, she would pray also – pray for Robert's safety – and for their little baby. Jessie's eyes sprang open. "The baby?" She glanced quickly around at those assembled but found only reassuring looks.

"She's fine," Lillian said gently.

"Jeff – Dr. Peters," Jamie corrected herself, "is with her. I was just in there myself and she's doing really well – especially considering how premature she was."

An intense longing rose in Jessie's heart. "I wish I could see her," she whispered. "What does my daughter look like?"

Lillian smiled at her. "She's got her father's green eyes and bright red hair."

Jessie sighed and closed her eyes, imagining what her daughter might look like.

When she opened her eyes again, the others had gone; only David remained.

Jessie turned toward him and was surprised to see the look of consternation on his face.

"Who is this red-haired Robert guy, Jessie?"

The weariness had returned to his voice and she didn't have the heart to rebuff him. "His name is Robert Carmichael," she began. "His parents are Irish. There are five younger children and three of the five have red hair."

David shook his head. "It's not the hair."

"They're good people," she protested. "They're not rich – like we are." Jessie's voice was edged with steel now. "Our mother wouldn't approve. I know that. But this is my life, David."

Her brother sighed. "Yes, it's your life. But you've always been able to have whatever you've wanted whenever you wanted it. Now tell me – exactly how poor are these people?"

Tears sprang to her eyes. "You're wrong, David! You're so wrong!"

"Jessie." His voice softened. "You don't realize –"

"No! You don't realize!" Jessie cried out. "I've never had anything that I wanted. I would have traded all the clothes and concert tickets and trips to Europe and – and everything if I could have just had one person – just one…" her voice trailed into a whisper "…to love me."

"Jess." He took her hand. Jessie felt the bandage.

"But you weren't there, David," she whispered. "And now you're getting married. And – and so am I."

The slow nod was not so much one of acquiescence as of resignation. She heard it in his voice, too. "So tell me about this fellow that you're planning to marry."

"He hasn't actually asked me yet," Jessie said shyly, "but I know he will. He said that he'd found an apartment and some furniture."

David sighed and sank back into the easy chair. Jessie looked at him in alarm. Did he really not want to hear? But David waved her on, a weary smile on his lips.

"He has such a wonderful family," Jessie began. "There is always so much laughter – and love. At bedtime, Mr. Carmichael takes each of the younger children on his lap and talks to them. They all get a kiss and hug from both parents. Robert and his sister Ashley both have their special times with their father, too. When Ashley's ready to go to bed, she'll come and sit with him for a few minutes and then later Robert will have his turn. They'll sit and have a cup of tea together and talk about their day or discuss this or that. Mrs. Carmichael is always there whenever one of her kids needs her. Of course, they can't believe that we call our mother by her first name and that I sometimes go weeks or even months without seeing her."

There was no response from David. Jessie leaned back into her pillow and continued talking. "I stayed there a few times. Cara never minded. I was out of her hair – that's all she ever cared about. But the Carmichaels – they were different. It was as if when I was there, I was just like one of their daughters. I helped with the dishes and sometimes read a story to the little ones. If they were going somewhere special, I was always invited to come along – even if it was to visit Robert's grandparents or his Uncle Joe.

"Robert's father and his Uncle Joe own a garage. Robert has worked there after school and during the summer for the last couple of years. He enjoys mechanics, and it's been enough to support the Carmichael family through the years. I know it would be enough for us too. David, I know we could be happy, Robert and I."

Jessie turned toward him. His eyes were still closed, but this time his face was in repose and his breathing was deep and regular. David had fallen asleep.

Jessie smiled. Well, some parts she might have to tell over again.

It was very quiet in the room. The door was partially closed, muffling sounds from the hallway. Rain continued to fall steadily, making tapping noises on the window.

Jessie thought about Robert and hoped that he was safe and dry inside somewhere. But why hadn't they found him yet? Where could he be?

It was a sound in the hallway that interrupted Jessie's thoughts and caused her to turn away from the window. A woman using a scolding tone alternated between English and the same language that Pipe had used. Jessie recognized Colin's voice replying but didn't understand his words.

Then she heard a third voice, and her heart leaped within her. *Robert!*

"I just have to see her!"

And then he was at the door.

Jessie's heart did another flip-flop as she gazed at him. His clothes were dripping wet and there was a wild urgency in his eyes. All she could think about was that he was safe and that he was here with her.

She wanted him to let go of the door and move closer. But he was holding onto it as if he might fall, staring at her with that look of wild desperation and breathing hard as if he'd been running.

"You're okay then," he finally gasped.

"Yes," she whispered.

He spun around and she heard his hoarse cry echoing down the hallway: "The baby!"

"She's okay!" Jessie called but knew he was too far gone to hear her.

"They'll tell him."

Jessie blinked. One dripping wet, young man had been replaced by another. But Colin was as calm as Robert had been distraught.

"He stayed with us last night," Colin explained, walking slowly into the room.

"Us?"

"Grandpa Pipe." Colin stopped at the foot of Jessie's bed. "I'm sorry that we frightened you. Robert and I talked until it was light out and Grandpa Pipe woke up and shooed us to bed. He didn't want to wake us so he didn't turn on the radio."

None of it was making sense to Jessie. "Why you? Why did he go to you?"

Colin shook his head. "I – couldn't sleep. I'd been sleeping most of the day after – after you…"

"After I went through the ice and you risked your life to save me," Jessie said softly. "I haven't had a chance to thank you."

Colin shrugged his shoulders and looked away.

"So you found Robert wandering the streets in the middle of the night."

Colin nodded, looking relieved to have the topic of conversation on someone besides himself. "He was a stranger – and he looked like he needed help."

"Thanks, Colin."

He nodded, his face relaxing into the lopsided grin that Jessie had come to associate with him. "I should go find Robert," he said, moving toward the door.

"Colin," Jessie stopped him. "Why is Robert so upset?"

"The radio; they gave a description of him and said that if anyone had seen this person, they should notify the police or come immediately to the hospital. Robert assumed the worst."

"He'll know by now that we're okay," Jessie mused.

Colin raised an eyebrow and quipped, "Now, I'll go make sure that *he's* okay."

Jessie's smile followed him out the door.

It was several minutes later when Colin reappeared, this time followed by Jamie, who was pushing an empty wheelchair.

"He's holding your baby," Colin explained, "and he'd like if you could join him."

"They let him?" Jessie burst out excitedly. "They'll let me?"

"Yes – and yes," Jamie answered with a smile as she reached for a housecoat for Jessie. Then her attention was drawn toward David, still fast asleep in the easy chair beside her bed. "I'm glad he's finally getting some rest."

Jamie got her to take it slow getting up, sitting on the edge of the bed for a moment before making the transfer to her wheelchair. Jessie was surprised to find how weak she still felt. The hospital gown and housecoat only came to her knees, so Jamie tucked a blanket around her legs. "I feel like an old woman," Jessie said ruefully.

"Well, you don't look like an old woman," Jamie reassured her.

"Oh, my hair!" Jessie exclaimed.

"Hmm, I guess you are getting better," Jamie said with a grin. But she found a brush and fixed Jessie's hair for her and gave her a cloth to wash her hands and face with. She even offered Jessie a piece of gum to freshen her breath.

"Do I look okay?" Jessie still worried.

"You look beautiful," Jamie reassured her.

They were by the door. Jessie glanced up at Colin. "Yeah, what she said," he quipped, moving to take Jamie's place pushing the wheelchair.

"You know where the nursery is?" she asked him.

Colin must have nodded in the affirmative because Jamie left them then.

There was no one else in the hallway. They passed an examination room. A nurse, with her back turned to them, was refilling a soap dispenser above the sink. There was another open door to a room that looked like an office; two closed doors indicated ladies' and men's bathrooms; and a supply room was beyond that.

But finally they came to the glass walls of the nursery.

She saw him before he saw her; Robert's entire focus was on the little bundle in his arms.

It was an incongruous sight. Robert was sitting in an old-fashioned wooden rocking chair holding their daughter, who was wrapped in a soft wool blanket. But he had changed into doctor's scrubs, and they were surrounded by beeping and hissing machinery with wires and tubes protruding from the little pink blanket.

She didn't notice Jeff approach them and was a little startled when he said, "You can come in, Jessie."

But it was Colin who hesitated by the door. As he pushed the chair further in, Jeff spoke to him as well. "You'll need to get out of those wet clothes. I'll find you another pair of scrubs."

Jessie barely noticed them leaving. Robert had raised his head and was looking at her. But the desperation and despair were gone. There was a calm, quiet confidence and an abiding love that shone from his eyes now, warming her heart and drawing her still nearer.

Jessie leaned forward, and Robert moved slightly so that she could have a better look at their child.

Jessie wasn't sure what she had expected. But it was a shock. She was so thin! And the oxygen mask made her little pinched face look even more pathetic. The shock of red hair seemed the only real, tangible thing on this tiny white figure, and it seemed almost too vivid – too real.

"She's going to be okay," Robert reassured her softly. "The doctor said so. She's going to grow up strong and healthy – with a fiery temper like her mom."

Jessie tried to smile, but tears were falling as well.

"She'll play in the sandbox in our backyard and we'll push her on a tire swing that we'll hang from a big oak tree," Robert continued in a slow, steady voice. "We'll teach her how to play baseball and," Robert grinned, "maybe I'll even teach her how to fix a car."

Jessie laughed, feeling the tensions of the last days and weeks melt away. She reached out a hand and gently touched her sleeping daughter's brow. "What should we call her?"

For the first time there was hesitancy in Robert's voice. "I was thinking maybe we could call her Hannah."

Jessie brushed a hand lightly over the fiery red hair. "Hannah."

Chapter Ten

"She looks pretty comfortable there." Jeff's voice sounded warm and friendly. "But maybe Mom would like to hold her for a minute."

"Yeah." Robert moved too quickly and startled the baby.

"Gently," Jeff said, easing the baby out of Robert's arms and into Jessie's.

Robert was apologetic. "You should have been the first to hold her."

"It's okay." Jessie smiled up at him. "You're her daddy." Then her eyes returned to her daughter. The blanket had fallen away a little and Jessie could see where some of the wires and tubes were attached.

She looked up at Jeff and said, "Please tell me about all these."

He stooped down beside her and carefully explained what had been done and what each piece of machinery was doing for her child. "We're mostly monitoring her. There's a lot that we can do but there's a lot…" He hesitated. "There's a lot that's in the Lord's hands, Jessie."

"So we should pray," Robert declared.

"Yes," Jessie breathed.

"Come and join us, Colin," Robert invited.

Colin squatted down beside Jeff, forming a circle of four around the baby. Jessie smiled at him. Colin – neither she nor her daughter would have been here if weren't for him.

Each of them prayed: Jeff with maturity and confidence, Jessie haltingly, Colin in a barely audible voice, and Robert with passionate urgency. But Jessie knew that each prayer had been sincere and each prayer had been heard.

Colin was invited to hold the baby for a moment before Jeff settled her back into the little incubator. Her oxygen mask was removed, but so was her blanket, no longer necessary in the heat-controlled environment. To Jessie, her little girl looked more tiny and frail than ever.

"She's going to be okay, Jess." Robert's voice and the hand he laid gently on her shoulder were a comfort to her, but suddenly fatigue swept over her once more and Jessie knew that she'd had all she could handle for the moment.

"I need to lie down."

Robert's response was immediate and once again apologetic. "I should have thought. You've been through so much. We've tired you out."

"Robert." Jessie touched his arm. "I wouldn't have missed any of this – not for the world."

He nodded and his face broke into a wide smile. "Me neither."

"So how are we doing?" Jamie's cheery nurse's voice carried across the room.

"We were just getting ready to go back to her room," Robert said. Then he turned toward Jeff and shook his hand. "Thank you, doctor."

Jeff took his hand but patted him on the back as well. "You can call me Jeff. You're going to be part of the family soon." He smiled at Robert's obvious confusion. "My sister is marrying Jessie's brother. That oughta make us some kind of relations."

"Yeah, I guess it does." He paused. "We'll get around to meeting everyone but for now..."

"Mm-hmm, let's go," Jamie agreed, "and maybe you can help me talk this girl into eating a few bites of lunch."

But Jessie knew she was much too tired for that.

She was glad for Jamie's help once again to get back into bed, and after a few sips of juice and a bite of toast, Jessie asked to have her bed lowered so that she could sleep.

Jamie left but soon after, Jessie could once more hear voices.

"I'm heading over to the lodge for a while," Colin was saying in his quiet, almost monotone voice. "If you need anything, let me know."

"Sure. Thanks," Robert answered, "Hey, you have your own duds back and they're dry. How'd you do that?"

"Jeff threw our stuff in the dryer. Yours is down there, too." There was a slight pause and a low chuckle. "You look like a doctor – maybe they'll let you stay in here longer, eh?"

"Right," Robert drawled. "Hey, take care buddy. I owe you a lot. You – and David. If you hadn't gone in there…"

Jessie could almost see Colin's crooked grin and casual shrug.

She wondered if David was still sleeping. He must be. Robert was settling into a chair on the other side of her bed. Jessie let herself drift off into a sweet dream of a little red-haired girl walking hand in hand between her daddy and mommy.

"This is so typical of her. David, honestly you have no idea what raising a teenage girl is like. She's been so moody this past year. And now this!"

"Cara," came the patient reply, "please keep your voice down. She's getting some much-needed rest."

"Why should I have consideration for her? She's certainly had none for me. It was difficult enough for me to reschedule the photo shoot because of your wedding. Then this! They did everything but get down on their knees and beg me, but I told them, 'After all, she is my daughter – my own flesh and blood.' And you did say that it was extremely urgent. Although she seems fine now that I'm here."

"Cara, there's no smoking allowed inside the health center."

"It's raining out, if you haven't noticed. What I really need is a good stiff drink, but I don't expect there's anything like that around here."

"No, but I could get you some hot tea or coffee – or probably even some hot chocolate."

"I'm not a child, David. I think I'll pass on the cocoa and cookies."

"Do you still like your coffee black?"

David must have left. Jessie heard only an impatient sigh and the clicking of her mother's heels on the tile floor. She was pacing back and forth by the foot of Jessie's bed. Cigarette smoke filled the air.

Then the footsteps stopped.

"Oh, you must be an orderly. Maybe you could help me. Maybe you could tell me why my mobile phone isn't working? Is there poor reception in this building or something?"

"I'm not an orderly but –"

"Not an orderly! Then what are you? It's a little early for Halloween."

"I was holding my baby in the nursery. I decided just to keep these clothes on so that I could go back and visit her –"

"And I suppose you have a very good reason for walking uninvited into my daughter's room?"

"Your daughter!"

Her eyelids felt like lead, but Jessie willed them to open. Robert.

"Your daughter." His voice trembled a little, but he steadied it and Jessie could see the strength and determination in his eyes. "I love your daughter and I intend to marry her."

Cara advanced until she was inches away from him. Cigarette still between her fingers, she shook her hand in his face. "I see what this is all about. The big crisis that I turned down twenty grand for! You got my daughter pregnant; you weren't man enough to help her take care of it; and now you think I'll let you ruin her entire life so you two can play house."

Jessie felt the blow as if Cara had slapped her instead of Robert. "No!" she cried out and tried to rise up in bed.

But David had arrived. "That's quite enough, Cara," he said firmly. "We need to talk. There's an office down the hall." He bent to pick up the cigarette that had flown out of her hand when she'd struck Robert.

"They're still children," Cara said through gritted teeth. "They think they can play this adult game. They have *no idea* what they're getting into!"

David's voice was weary but still held resolve. "It was a long trip. You're tired. Come and have a cup of coffee."

She was walking toward the door, following his lead. "How could she have kept that a secret from me? She can't possibly leave school. I won't have a high school dropout in the family."

Her voice faded down the hallway.

Robert remained where he was, a large red spot on his left cheek, partially overlapping a day-old bruise.

Jessie's was choked with tears. "Robert."

He came slowly toward her, his eyes still downcast. "Maybe she's right," he mumbled.

"No!" Jessie cried.

He raised his eyes a little to meet hers.

"No," she said again, this time opening her arms to him.

He bent over her, and she held him tightly as he said in a tear-filled voice, "Jessie, I don't know if I can…"

"We're in this together," she said.

He raised his face towards hers. "I love you, Jess. I love you so much."

"I love you, Robert."

He shut his eyes and shook his head. "I've let you down, Jess. We should have waited. We were having fun – and then things got complicated."

Jessie nodded. "I guess I thought maybe I could hang onto you more if we were – physically involved."

"No." Robert shook his head sadly. "It just about ended our relationship – especially after I became a Christian. I thought maybe it would be best if we just broke it off – if I didn't see you ever again."

"But you didn't break it off," Jessie whispered.

"No." Robert grinned. "You had me by then – hook, line and sinker!"

Jessie smiled but had to ask, "Any regrets?"

He bent to tenderly kiss her before answering. "None."

"You're not marrying me because of the baby?"

"No." He shook his head. "I'm marrying you because of your smile and because of your spunk and –"

"Spunk?" Jessie asked incredulously.

Robert laughed as he rose from his knees and dropped into the chair beside her bed. "I guess I knew that life with you would never be boring," he said.

Jessie had to laugh, too. *Spunk!*

"Well, that sounds better!" David said entering the room. "Actually the best prescription I could give you."

Jessie and Robert turned toward him as he quoted, "A glad heart is good medicine – Proverbs 17:22."

"Where's Cara?" Jessie asked.

"I got her settled in with Jenny – Jeff's wife." David sank down into the easy chair with a deep sigh. "They have a beautiful house – Cara will be impressed. And Jenny is a great hostess."

David looked over at Robert. "I'm sorry about all this. You've had a pretty lousy reception from the Rodriguez family."

Robert stroked his jaw. "Are there – uh – any more of you?"

"No." David grinned. "That's the lot of us."

"Dad," Jessie whispered.

David shook his head dismissively. "Her – our – father – he left shortly after – about eighteen years ago. He wasn't around much before that, but we only hear from him about once a year now – a card at Christmas signed by his new wife, usually full of news about their kids. I guess he's a good dad to them; I don't know."

Jessie felt Robert take hold of her hands and was grateful. They were cold – ice cold.

"And *that's* the lot of us," she said.

"No grandparents – or aunts or uncles?"

Jessie shook her head. "Cara wasn't much interested in staying in touch with family. I don't think she was exactly ashamed of them but she wanted a different kind of life, I guess. And we traveled a lot."

"Cara – I still find it strange that you call your mother by her first name," Robert said.

"That's the way it was even when I was a small child," David said. "Her modeling and intermittent acting career always came first. She'd always lie about her age and quite often she would refer to us as her younger siblings instead of as her children."

"We always had nannies," Jessie continued. "I don't think Cara was ever very comfortable with the role of mother."

Robert's voice was hesitant as he asked, "Would you want to have a nanny for our baby, Jessie?"

"Never!" she declared then, suddenly remembering, exclaimed, "Oh, David! I got to hold her. I got to hold Hannah!"

"Hannah?"

Jessie smiled at Robert and took his hand. "That's what we called her – Hannah."

David stroked his chin, pursed his lips and nodded his head emphatically. "I like it."

Hurried footsteps sounded in the hallway. "David!" Jamie called urgently from the doorway. "We need your help; Jeff's with another patient."

David hurried after her without a backward glance, and Jessie and Robert were left alone once more.

"I really like the name, too," Jessie said. "How did you come up with it?"

Robert grinned shyly. "I was waiting in the airport in Toronto and looking for something to read. There was this little book with baby's names and their meanings."

Jessie was deeply touched that he would be thinking about their baby to the extent of even choosing names. "And what does Hannah mean?" she asked softly.

Robert leaned forward, his eyes sparkling, "It means 'He has favored me' or 'God has been gracious to me.'" Robert's voice deepened with intensity. "And God has been gracious to me – blessing me with you and with Hannah."

Tears clouded Jessie's eyes. "But you didn't know then..."

Robert took her hand. "No," he agreed, "I didn't know then. When I called to speak with you and they wouldn't let me, I kind of panicked. I just dropped everything and got on a plane. The Lord kept quieting my heart, bringing Bible verses to mind, and it was during one of those times that I was thinking of God's grace. But my imagination still kept running wild."

Robert dropped his eyes as he continued. "When you told me you were pregnant and I said I needed time, you left in such a hurry and you seemed so angry I was afraid you would do something drastic. Then when I heard that your brother was a doctor, I thought maybe you would try to arrange something through him."

"I wanted to," Jessie whispered.

Robert closed his eyes and nodded slowly. Unconsciously, his hand withdrew from hers. "When I got here and they told me you were at the clinic, I thought abortion clinic – which is just nuts because we're way up here in the wilds of Northern Canada."

"We still came so close to losing her," Jessie said, tears streaming down her face.

"Yes," he whispered hoarsely, clasping her hand once more and drawing her eyes back to him, "but God was gracious."

"Yes," she breathed.

A look of wonder came over his face. "Jess – are you – I mean – have you…?"

Laughter bubbled up within her. "Yes, I am – and yes, I have!"

"But how? When?" He shook his head in amazement. "You were so – angry."

Jessie glanced down and then back up again, joy replacing shame in that brief moment. "I guess it was when I finally understood that God loves me – that He will never let me down – that He will be like the daddy eagles –"

Robert laughed. "What?"

"Daddy eagles," Jessie explained excitedly. "They swoop down under their babies and lift them up. They can actually dive faster than the baby can fall. It's kind of part of the mating contract that they're good swoopers."

Robert could hardly speak because he was laughing so hard. "Good swoopers!"

"Yes." Jessie rolled her eyes. "You can even ask Colin's grandpa if you don't believe me."

"Pipe," Robert said respectfully, a quiet smile replacing laughter.

"You know him."

Robert nodded. "We talked for a long time last night, the three of us. He has a lot of wisdom. Colin, too."

Jessie nodded as Robert continued. "He found me out wandering around the streets. I had no idea where the hotel was and there's a distinctly unfriendly feeling about this place at three in the morning – gangs of kids, high on something and just looking for trouble.

"Jess," he broke off, "I can't tell you how happy I am that you're a Christian now."

Jessie smiled. "I'm happy, too."

Robert bent to kiss her. But Jessie's eye caught a flash of movement by the door. Oh no, not again!

Robert followed her gaze and with a deep sigh sank back onto the chair and lowered his eyes. Jessie looked up at David. He didn't look so much angry this time as just simply worn out.

"You said that you'd seen and held your baby?" David asked her.

"Yes," Jessie answered in a bare whisper.

"And you?" He cast his eyes in Robert's direction.

Jessie felt a cold fear seeping into her heart, but Robert's reaction was more explosive. He jumped out of the chair, his voice trembling and chest heaving. "What's wrong with her? What's wrong with our baby? Why are you asking if we've held her?"

But David was wearily waving him back into his seat. "She's stable again." He advanced into the room. "I just don't know for how long. She's had another setback."

His voice seemed to just fade out as if he was too weary to continue.

Robert expelled a deep breath, stared at David for an instant, then took his arm and led him toward the easy chair beside Jessie's bed. "I'll get you some coffee – or tea – or something."

David rubbed his forehead. "Tea," he mumbled. "Ask Lillian."

Robert left the room and Jessie turned to speak to her brother. "Have *you* had a chance to hold her?" she asked gently.

Jessie saw him flinch and wished she could withdraw the question. It was as if she'd touched an open wound. David's voice held a tinge of bitterness that surprised Jessie. "I've cut her, sutured her, suctioned her, poked her heel so many times that it looks like a pin cushion." He drew in a deep breath. "But no, I haven't got to hold her yet."

"David!" Jessie gasped.

"I'm sorry." He lifted a trembling hand to his forehead. "I'm too close to this case. I shouldn't be your doctor. Maybe we should Med-i-vac her out to Winnipeg. They have an excellent neonatal unit –"

"That won't be necessary." Jeff Peters's voice sounded from the doorway. "Doctor Tanabe is arriving on the afternoon flight today. He can assist and relieve me. I'll be on twenty-four-hour call until you're able to resume duties again. Now, go home and get some rest!"

Chapter Eleven

Robert expressed surprise at finding David gone but seemed grateful that Jeff was available to answer his many questions. They talked at length about the various medical problems that Hannah was encountering. Jessie interjected an occasional question, but it was as if her heart were too full to really take in all the medical terms and procedures, even though Jeff was trying to make it as simple as possible.

She was glad when Robert finally cut to the chase and asked the question foremost in Jessie's mind: "Dr. Peters – Jeff – what are Hannah's chances? What we really need to know is if she's – if she's going to make it?"

Jeff nodded understandingly; he anticipated the question. He answered with a voice that was calm and clear but also filled with compassion. "At this point, your daughter has a slightly better than average chance of survival. If you had asked me a half-hour ago, I would have given you a much worse prognosis. But she's weathered this crisis – somewhat successfully – and we can have reasonable hope that she will continue to progress, perhaps even above our present expectations."

"Can I see her?" Jessie whispered.

Jeff smiled kindly. "Yes, you can. Would you like to try walking?"

Jessie nodded eagerly and managed to sit up by herself and stand unassisted. Jeff voiced his approval and suggested that perhaps the IV could be removed – as long as she kept up her fluid intake. Jessie sat on the edge of the bed as Jeff continued. "I could probably discharge you into my mother's care since she's a nurse, but I think you might rather be close to your baby at this time."

"Yes!" Jessie spoke fervently.

"We have an apartment of sorts at the other end of the health center. It's especially designed for situations such as this. Families can stay there as long as the patient is in critical condition." Jeff nodded thoughtfully. "It might be for the best if we kept an eye on you for a day or two more as well."

He checked her vital signs before removing the IV, wrote something in her chart, and promised to send a nurse in later to help her move.

Robert was looking happy. He stood to his feet to shake Jeff's hand and thank him. Jeff nodded and smiled at both of them before turning to go. Jessie felt a rush of joy and a tingle of excitement. It was good to be released from care. There was a feeling of renewed hope as well; if she was getting well herself, maybe her daughter was too.

They spent the rest of the evening by Hannah's side, watching the tiny chest rise and fall. She would open her eyes occasionally and once even seemed to be looking at them.

"Hannah," Robert said tenderly, touching his daughter's hand through the incubator. "You need to be strong. You need to fight. We want to hold you in our arms but you need to get well first."

"She has such beautiful eyes," Jessie said, "and lovely long lashes."

Robert grinned, "Yeah, she's gonna be a real knockout. We'll have the boys lined up outside our door." Jessie rolled her eyes as he continued, "We'll have to get a second phone line put in."

"Robert!" Jessie protested with a laugh. "I think we don't have to worry about that quite yet."

"No." He spoke soberly, looking down at Hannah once more. "First we gotta get you better." Then without preamble, he began praying, "Dear Jesus, please heal our little girl. We really love her and we want her to stay with us. But whatever your will is, we trust you Jesus. Just – just give us the strength we need…"

No! Jessie's heart cried. *I don't want His will – I want my baby!*

"…In Jesus name, Amen."

Jessie asked in a trembling voice, "Can't God heal her?"

Jessie saw the tears in his eyes as he turned his face toward hers. "Of course He can, Jess," he said gently, "but He knows what's best. He'll do what's best – for all of us. He loves us – and we can trust Him."

Can I? Jessie wondered. *Can I trust Him?*

Jamie came just before her shift was over to settle Jessie into her new room. Colin came by to ask if Robert would like to stay with them for the night again and Robert was finally persuaded to leave after he was assured that he would be called if there was any change at all in Hannah's condition. Since there was no phone at the cabin, Jamie promised him that someone would drive down immediately to the cabin and bring him back if he was needed.

Jessie didn't sleep well that night and wandered frequently down to the nursery to check on Hannah. The nurses were understanding and always tried to make her feel comfortable and answer her questions. Hannah seemed to at least be holding her own and perhaps even getting a little better.

Morning finally arrived, and with the morning came visitors. The little suite had a small bedroom with a hospital bed; a bathroom with toilet, sink, and shower; and a sitting room with a fold-away sofa, an easy chair, and a small kitchen table and chairs. Jessie had opened the curtains and the sun was streaming in.

Robert was the first to arrive, checking on Hannah before coming to Jessie's room at a little after seven. He was followed by Coralee and David; Jessie was pleased to see that her brother looked rested and much more like himself again.

"Are you here as a doctor – or just as my brother?" she asked.

"*Just* your brother?" David quipped with a raised eyebrow.

Jessie sighed theatrically. "What I meant was…"

David punched her lightly in the shoulder. "I know what you meant, kiddo. Actually," he said in a more serious tone, "Jeff and Dr. Tanabe are handling things quite well. I'd forgotten that he was due to replace me for a few days anyway." He took Coralee's hand. "Today was going to be our wedding day."

Jessie drew in a breath. "I'm sorry, David."

"Hey," he said lightly, "nothing to be sorry about. We're still getting married. A day or two won't make much difference."

"Actually," Coralee put in, "we're glad you're both here. We need to talk to you about *your* plans."

Jessie and Robert exchanged glances. Their hands drew naturally together. "Whenever you're ready, Jess," he said gently. "I'd marry you this minute if I could."

"Not in this hospital gown!" Jessie laughed.

"Oh, I nearly forgot!" Coralee reached for the bag she had set down beside her. "I heard they'd moved you over here. I brought you some clothes."

"Thanks!" Jessie smiled gratefully. "Do you mind if I change?" Jessie hurried to the bathroom and put on her own clothes. She'd already had a shower and was feeling much less tired and sore than she had the day before – almost back to normal. Coralee had put some makeup in the bag as well, and Jessie took her time applying it.

A knock sounded on the bathroom door. "Hey, hurry up in there!" David called. "We're growing old and gray out here waiting for you."

Jessie put on a final touch of lip gloss and opened the door. She rolled her eyes at David before turning with mock exasperation to Coralee. "He used to do this all the time at home! He never let me have the bathroom. Just be forewarned – after you get married, plan to have at least two bathrooms!"

Coralee laughed and turned toward David. "Is that right?" she drawled.

Robert had been silent. His eyes were fixed upon Jessie as if seeing her for the first time. "You're so beautiful," he said softly.

Jessie moved toward him, forgetting everyone else, thinking only of him.

"About that wedding…"

Jessie shook her head, exchanged grins with Robert and settled in beside him on the couch before fluttering her eyelids toward her brother. "Yes?"

"Sorry to destroy the romantic moment," David said with a broad grin, "but maybe you guys could come back down to earth for a minute."

"I'm all ears," Jessie assured him.

David's smile faded. "Actually," he said, "it's Cara; she's getting real anxious to leave."

"She just got here!" Robert exclaimed.

"You've got to understand Cara –" David began.

"Her career is very important to her," Jessie said.

Robert looked ready to say something else, but David interjected. "Which is why I wanted to talk to you guys."

He looked from one to the other. "How would you feel if we had the wedding today? You'd be only a phone call away. We could get from the lodge to the hospital in less than five minutes."

"Sure," Jessie quickly agreed.

"Absolutely," Robert added.

"You have everything ready." Jessie leaned forward to pat David's knee. "You should continue with the wedding as planned."

Coralee said hesitantly, "We were hoping that you would join us."

Robert nodded his agreement. "Count me in. As long as Jessie doesn't have to stand too long. She's one of your bridesmaids, isn't she?"

David exhaled, and exchanged a quick look with Coralee. "What we mean," he said slowly, "is that we would not be opposed to the idea of a double wedding – if that's what you also want."

"Oh!" Jessie squealed with delight and hugged her brother but turned quickly back toward Robert when she realized he had remained silent.

Fear clutched Jessie's heart as she searched his face. He was avoiding her eyes. Had he changed his mind? Her thoughts flashed back, trying to remember: had he even asked her? Was her idea of marriage all one-sided?

"Thank you for the offer," Robert began, his attention focused on David, "but –"

Jessie held her breath. *But what?*

"But I would really like my family to be present," Robert finished quietly.

Jessie exhaled; Coralee said, "Of course you do;" and David said, "We understand."

Robert glanced quickly at Jessie before turning his attention back to David. "They could probably be here in a day or two – depending on how quickly we could arrange transportation – but there's no way they can reach here today. They were planning to come up anyway." He turned to Jessie. "Both times they called, you were sleeping, but they wanted me to tell you that they are thinking about you – and praying for you. And Mom especially is anxious to see her granddaughter."

"What will they think about us getting married?" Jessie asked.

Robert grinned. "They'll be delighted. I had a long talk with Dad yesterday. I told him that we were engaged and he gave me a lot of fatherly advice – a part of which was that we should get married as soon as possible."

"Your dad said that?" Jessie asked in amazement.

Robert smiled and nodded.

Jessie hugged him. "You have such an awesome family!"

"We could help with the transportation," David volunteered.

"And maybe we could persuade Cara to stay an extra day or two since she'll be marrying off both of her children at the same time," Coralee added.

"A real bargain," Jessie said with a tinge of bitterness in her voice. "Even her agent would have to agree it's a time saver!"

"Jess," Robert said softly.

Jessie tucked her feet up on the couch and let him draw her closer. "David," she said from the comfort of Robert's arms, "Daddy said 'no' to coming to your wedding. Do you think he'd come if we were both getting married?"

David shook his head and turned away. This time it was Coralee's turn to comfort him. "We could at least ask," she said gently.

"We could ask," he agreed wearily.

"Hey," Robert said cheerfully, "we have a lot of work to do; we should get started."

David rallied to the occasion. "We'll check out flights and connections first – see how soon we can get your family up here."

"And I think I should talk to your mother," Robert added ruefully, rubbing his cheek. "Our first meeting didn't go all that well."

"You want me to go with you, buddy?" David offered.

But Robert shook his head. "Thanks anyway."

"Well," David said, "Cara won't be up for at least anther two hours so why don't we call your parents first and get things going from that end?"

They put the call through from the room Jessie was in and she was able to talk to Robert's parents as well. They were happy that she was doing better but concerned that Hannah was still struggling.

"We'd like to come up there, dear," Mrs. Carmichael told Jessie. "You shouldn't be alone at a time like this."

"I'm not alone," Jessie said but then immediately felt an overwhelming urge to have Mrs. Carmichael's strong, loving arms around her.

"Let me talk to her," Jessie heard Mr. Carmichael's voice in the background.

"Jessie," his voice boomed, "how're you holding up, my girl?"

"I'm fine, Mr. C." Jessie tried to sound brave – but her voice shook and tears were forming in her eyes.

"We're all packed and ready to come up there; you just say the word. Hey, let me talk to that son of mine."

Jessie handed the phone to Robert. "Your dad."

"We'll go to the airport and see what we can arrange," David whispered as he and Coralee rose to go.

Robert nodded and continued to talk to his father. Their conversation had turned to transportation as well. Jessie leaned her head on Robert's shoulder and imagined herself in the Carmichael kitchen. "Clean enough to be healthy; messy enough to be happy," was how Mrs. C. always described her kitchen. There always seemed to be something in progress there – soup on the back of the stove or cookies in the oven. Jessie could almost smell the sweet odors and feel the warmth as Robert continued to talk with his dad. He put his hand over the receiver and spoke to Jessie. "Mom wants to know if you need a wedding dress and would like to borrow hers?"

Jessie, momentarily stunned, finally stammered, "Yes – tell her yes, thank you."

Robert relayed the message to his dad, who relayed it to his wife. "She wants to talk to you, Jess," Robert said, holding the receiver out to her.

"I've had it put away very carefully, so it should still be in very good condition," Mrs. Carmichael told her. "It should fit you, dear. I was actually quite small in my younger years."

A vision of Mrs. Carmichael rose in Jessie's mind. "Pleasantly plump" was what she always called herself. Jessie assured her that the dress would probably fit and if not, maybe Jamie could make some quick adjustments.

"Well, dear, we should be going," the older woman spoke hurriedly, "There's a direct flight into Pearson International Airport in Toronto, Canada. We can just make it if we hurry. Take care of yourself, Jessie. Get lots of rest. You have a big day ahead of you. And take care of that little granddaughter of mine. We love you. Bye now."

Jessie hung up the phone with a smile on her face. With Mr. and Mrs. C. there, the wedding would be perfect.

Robert stood to his feet. "I should go find Colin. I'd like to ask him to be my best man."

Coralee and David walked in at that moment. "And who were you thinking of for a bridesmaid?" Coralee asked.

"Maybe one of Robert's sisters." She turned toward her fiancé. "Do you think Ashley would like to be my maid of honor?"

Robert smiled, "I'm sure she'd love to!"

"I think my dress might fit her," Jessie said.

"Is your whole family coming?" David asked of Robert.

"They wouldn't miss it for the world. Even my Uncle Joe is coming. Dad said it was the first time in eighteen years that they ever closed the shop in the middle of a workweek!"

"I've never even been to a double wedding before; we need to talk about logistics." Coralee sat gracefully in the easy chair and crossed one long leg over the other as she spoke.

David straddled the arm of her chair and grinned. "Shouldn't be too hard: we get hitched; they get hitched; and we all go home!"

Jessie rolled her eyes and turned her attention back to Coralee. "What do you think would work best?" she asked.

Coralee leaned forward and her voice grew excited. "Well, I was thinking; we could each come down one of the spiral staircases. Does David have a younger brother and sister that could be your ring bearer and flower girl? They'd need some fancy clothes."

"Tiffany loves to dress up," Jessie said, "and her mom usually does her hair up nice even for church. Tim would be about the same size as Bobby; maybe he could borrow something. But if I know Mrs. C., she'll have all the kids dressed up for the wedding. Even Mr. C. will have to squeeze himself into a suit if she's got anything to say about it!"

Robert chuckled as Coralee continued, "Don't worry about the flowers; we seem to have quite a lot of them and can easily make another bouquet. Missy was going to spread rose petals as we walked; Robert's sister – what's her name? – Tiffany – can do the same on the other spiral staircase for you."

David slid off the chair and sauntered toward the door. "Robert, what say we leave the ladies to discuss particulars and go find your best man?"

The pair left, leaving Coralee and Jessie to discuss dresses, flowers, and photos. Jessie grew more excited by the minute as her wedding gradually became more of a reality.

"David said that he'd help Robert with the license and everything," Coralee said. "We can use the same minister; I'm sure that he'll agree, especially after he meets you two and hears your story."

Chapter Twelve

But as it turned out, Pastor Thomas was not at all keen to marry two eighteen-year-olds!

It wasn't until he'd had lengthy talks with Jessie and Robert separately and then with them both together that he even considered the idea. He met with David for a while also but still wouldn't commit himself until he'd met Robert's family.

It was obvious that he was indeed touched by their story and rejoiced with them over their newfound faith, but he still felt it might be wise for them to wait a year or two. He was shaky on the logistics of how they would parent together during this time but felt this was important also.

Jessie, getting used to praying about her concerns, tried to leave it all in God's hands and not worry about it. Besides, she was confident that when Pastor Thomas met the Carmichael family, all his fears would be relieved.

Meanwhile, David had discussed rings with Robert and had helped him make the necessary arrangements to purchase a set from the same jewelry store in Toronto where he had bought his and Coralee's. The store manager agreed to have the rings waiting at the ticket agent's at Pearson International Airport that very morning so that Robert's parents could pick them up.

The license at first presented some difficulties, but David's friend Charles was a whiz at government regulations and could work wonders on the Internet, finding the necessary information and processing the paperwork.

Hannah was doing better than expected, and the doctors were pleased with her progress. Jessie got to hold her for a short time after lunch. David was with her, this time in the role of uncle instead of doctor.

Jenny stopped by to talk to Jessie about shoes but didn't stay long. "I need to be getting back," she said. "Cara is taking a nap but I want to be there for her when she wakes up."

"Be there for her?" Jessie looked at Jenny in surprise. In all her life she had never heard Cara referred to in such a way. Always, Cara had been totally self-absorbed but also totally self-sufficient. If she needed anything, she demanded it of whoever was currently available.

Jenny smiled understandingly. "Even the strongest of women need to lay aside their armor now and then. Your mother and I talked until almost three in the morning." Jenny hesitated, choosing her words carefully. "She throws a lot of barbs, but they're more of a defense than an offense. She's just never learned how to love or be loved."

Jessie glanced at David. He was staring open-mouthed at Jenny. It did seem a bit incredulous.

"She's…" Jenny hesitated once more, "she's not going to change overnight but I would like the opportunity of seeing her through this time. It must be a little earth-shaking to have both of your children getting married at the same time – and to find out that you're a grandmother twice over. She had no idea you were pregnant, Jess. And she's had to go through all this alone – without the support of a husband."

And whose fault is that? Jessie thought angrily.

"She wrote a rather large check this morning," Jenny continued, directing her comments to David now. "She wanted to help out with any extra expenses."

Jessie saw the paper pass from Jenny to David's hand and thought of all the hundreds of times when money had been exchanged on her behalf. But it wasn't money or possessions that she'd needed as a child; it was love.

The Carmichaels arrived in a whirlwind of enthusiasm and energy. They stopped in to see the baby then crowded into Jessie's room, filling it to bursting with their exuberant chatter. The girls were so excited they could hardly stand still. Ashley and Tiffany were thrilled to be in the wedding party; Tim was happy to be the ring bearer; and Robert's other brother, Brandon, wanted to know what he could be. Jessie consulted with Coralee and was told that Brandon could be head usher, a position he was proud to accept.

Pastor Thomas arrived and was warmly greeted by Mr. and Mrs. Carmichael. He expressed his concerns about the speed with which the young – very young – couple were going about things.

Mr. Carmichael nodded his head. "We would have liked them to have waited a while," he agreed. "But we aren't worried about their commitment to each other or about their ability to raise a child together. They won't be alone in this."

"After Robert graduates in June, he'll be spending eight hours a day with his dad," Mrs. Carmichael said. "And the apartment they'll be moving into is just two blocks from our house."

Jessie interjected, "I already spend most of my free time at the Carmichael house. The only way that will change is that some of that free time will be spent with them visiting us at our new apartment."

"And what about your schooling?" Pastor Thomas asked like a stern father, though he was only a young man himself.

Jessie grinned. "School's never been a problem for me. I'll graduate; don't worry."

Pastor Thomas said to Mr. and Mrs. Carmichael, "Well, as long as you promise your support and your blessing..."

"We do," they both said.

Satisfied, Pastor Thomas arranged a time for a meeting with the two couples to discuss the ceremony.

The party gradually moved over to the lodge. For Jessie, it felt great to be outside again, and it was wonderful to be swept along in this enthusiastic crowd of well-wishers.

Mrs. Carmichael and Martha hit it off right away, and the men naturally gravitated toward the fireplace to talk. Bobby invited the two boys to play a computer game with him, and the girls ran upstairs with Coralee, talking of hairstyles and dresses.

Jessie went to sit beside Robert on the sofa in front of the fireplace. She tucked her legs up and rested her head on his shoulder. The flames rose and fell, the wood crackled and snapped – and Jessie fell asleep.

They kept supper waiting for her as long as they could but finally wakened her. Jessie was a little embarrassed that people had been waiting for her but felt grateful nonetheless for their kindness and concern.

They had put several tables together to make one very long one. There were twenty-one of them altogether, not including the two babies. No seats were designated but people tended to sit down in couples. Cara was one of the last to arrive, stubbing out a cigarette at the far end of the lodge before joining the group. Everyone was talking happily as they arranged themselves around the table. Cara's snide remark was heard by only a few. "Quite the League of Nations here."

Jessie heard it and blushed. Robert was speaking to his father and didn't hear. Jessie saw Colin stiffen and rise to leave but Jeff put an arm on his shoulder and spoke something quietly. Jenny rose to guide Cara to a place that she had saved beside her and, ignoring her comment, started to talk about the beautiful flower arrangements on the table. Jeff caught Jessie's eye and smiled reassuringly at her, Ashley began to talk about the bridesmaid's dress, and Jessie relaxed and enjoyed her meal.

Jeff excused himself as soon as the meal was over and headed back to check on Hannah. Coralee got up to take care of baby Michael, and Jamie followed to take care of her daughter, Rosalee. The rest of the group dispersed soon after, the children heading off first and the adults gradually leaving as well.

Cara stated that she felt a migraine coming on, and Jenny offered to take her home. Jessie said goodnight to her mother, and David saw her to the door. A sense of relief flooded Jessie as the door closed behind her and David returned alone.

He grinned at her. "She took it pretty well, I'd say."

"She's had time to work things through," Jessie replied.

David shook his head. "She didn't know that Coralee is African-American."

Jessie could only stare at him. So David had withheld things, too!

Her thoughts were interrupted as Robert joined them, a broad smile on his face and a small velvet box in his hand. David placed a hand on his shoulder, winked at Jessie, and sauntered away. Robert led her to a love seat at the far end of the lodge, where they could be alone. Then he knelt on one knee and took her hand in his.

"I have never formally asked you to marry me, Jessie," he said, looking deep into her eyes.

Jessie's heart beat like a big bass drum. "But you know that my answer is yes," she whispered.

Robert opened the box and slipped one of the rings on her finger. His voice was husky with emotion. "I love you,

Jessie. I want to be your husband and I want you to be my wife."

"For always," Jessie affirmed.

"For always," he promised as he rose to kiss her gently on the lips.

They sat together on the love seat facing the glass doors leading out to a patio. It was almost dark, though it was barely seven o'clock. Robert's arm was around her and Jessie leaned her head on his shoulder.

"So what do you want to do on your very last night of being single?" he asked.

"Isn't there a lot to do – and get ready?"

Robert shook his head. "Mrs. Peters told me that we shouldn't worry at all. Especially now that Mom's here to help, they'll have no problem getting everything ready in time."

"I need to try on the wedding dress that your mom brought," Jessie said, "and I think Coralee said something about a rehearsal."

Robert grinned cheerfully. "Let's go find out!"

But Jessie reached out for his hand as he started to rise. "What I really want to do," she said softly, "is go back to the health center. I feel like part of me is missing."

"I feel that way, too," Robert quickly assured her. "Let's hurry and get done with what we have to do and then go straight on over there."

"I know Jeff would call us if there were any problems."

Robert nodded. "I'm sure he would."

The wedding dress, amazingly, didn't need any adjustments at all and the ladies all agreed that Jessie looked beautiful in it. Pastor Thomas walked them briefly through the wedding ceremony, and Coralee declared that everything else could wait for the morning. Martha asked Jessie if she had any special preferences about flowers or the table seating or anything else. "Only one preference," she answered, her eyes resting on Robert.

"Oh, we'll make sure you get the right bridegroom!" Coralee laughed.

"And I'll make sure I get the right bride!" Robert declared.

They left the lodge in high spirits. David drove them to the health center, where they found that Hannah was doing well. Jessie and Robert got to hold her for a while but then Jeff advised Jessie to get some sleep. David agreed with that. "You have a big day tomorrow, kiddo! You'd better get your beauty sleep!"

Jessie rolled her eyes and would have protested if she hadn't felt so tired! It had been a wonderful day – but an exhausting one as well.

Robert headed back to the lodge with David for a while, planning to leave with Colin for Pipe's cabin when they were ready to go to bed.

Jessie slept through the night and woke to a beautiful sunny day. By the time she was showered and dressed, and had checked in on Hannah, Coralee arrived to drive her over to the lodge. They would get ready in the upstairs bedrooms, and after everyone had arrived, the wedding would begin and they would make their grand entrance down the spiral staircases.

The Carmichaels had been guests of the Peters, spreading their large family over two of the cabins, and Mrs. C. was busy helping Martha with some finishing touches on the food. Jamie and Bill were there as well, Jamie fixing the little girl's hair and Bill arranging tables and chairs. Cara arrived, her headache obviously gone and her whole forceful personality prepared to dominate the proceedings. She declared it would be she who helped Jessie with her wedding dress. After all, she was the bride's mother!

She insisted on arranging the seating at the reception, instructing Jessie's bridesmaid, Ashley, how to make neat little place cards for each person. She almost threw a fit when Tom declared that they would toast the brides and grooms with fruit punch rather than an alcoholic beverage, but it turned out that she had met her match; Tom could be just as forcible as she could and this was one issue he was not about to budge on.

The wedding was set for ten o'clock. At nine-forty-five, Jessie and Coralee were ready, but Mrs. Carmichael, Jenny, and Jamie were still moving back and forth between the rooms doing finishing touches as needed. Martha was also supervising downstairs as the guests arrived and were seated. She came upstairs at a couple of minutes before ten to say that the bridegrooms and best men had arrived. Mrs. Carmichael was able to tell her that all the ladies and two ring bearers were also ready.

The mother's went down to be seated with the other guests. Jessie heard the music begin and the flower girls and ring bearers left the room, followed by the bridesmaids and finally the two brides.

As Jessie touched the top of the staircase, she glanced over at the other procession to time her descent with Coralee's. Jamie and Coralee were still at the top, waiting as Missy scattered rose petals on the steps and Bobby followed slowly behind. Jessie, watching the pair, felt a sudden lurch in her heart. These two, looking so wonderfully cute in long dress and suit, had been unwanted babies, rejected at birth.

But God had other plans for them.

Jamie began her descent. She had adopted another unwanted child, baby Rosalee.

Coralee started down the stairs, and Jessie began to walk down as well. Coralee and David would adopt baby Michael.

Jessie turned her focus toward the bottom of the spiral staircase where Robert stood waiting, gazing up at her. They too had a baby that had been initially unwanted. But now she was cherished by them both.

How Jessie wished that Hannah could be here with them. She smiled down at Robert. He would be a good husband, and he would be a good father to their precious baby daughter.

Robert took her hand as she reached the bottom of the stairs. His eyes remained on her as they moved slowly to take their positions in front of their family and friends.

The two couples stood close together, David and Jessie almost touching shoulders. The ceremony was conducted in sections, first for one couple and then for the other. There was the declaration of intent, the saying of vows, the kissing of the brides, and finally the announcement to the audience of the official union of Mr. and Mr. Rodriguez, and Mr. and Mrs. Carmichael. Spontaneous applause followed the two couples as they walked down the aisle between the chairs to form a greeting line by the trellis intertwined with flowers.

Two gift tables had been set up. Jessie was surprised to see quite a few gifts on the one set aside for her and Robert. But one person wished to give his to her personally. Grandpa Pipe's face was crinkled into a wide smile as he handed her a beautiful little wood carving that he told Jessie he had made himself just for her.

Jessie took it from his hand, smiled her thanks and gave him a big hug as well. But she couldn't speak; her heart was too full of joy for all that the Lord had done.

The carving was of an eagle with wings outspread. On its back a baby eaglet rested, confident and secure that her Father would never let her down.

For You made the parts inside me. You put me together inside my mother.

I will give thanks to You, for the greatness of the way I was made brings fear. Your works are great and my soul knows it very well.

My bones were not hidden from You when I was made in secret and put together with care in the deep part of the earth.

Your eyes saw me before I was put together. And all the days of my life were written in Your book before any of them came to be.

Psalm 139: 13–16

BOOKS BY DORENE MEYER

Rachel's Children (2012)
Jessie's Secret (2013)
Colin's Choice (2005, 2013)
Deep Waters (2007, 2008)
Pilot Error (2008, 2009)
Get Lost!(2006, 2007)
The Little Ones (2009)

Jasmine (2010)
Lewis (2011)
Joshua (2012)
Missy (2012)
Starla (2013)
Randi (2014)
Keegan (2014)